WHEN THE HUMMINGBIRDS DANCED IN A HONEYSUCKLE SKY

PATRICK E. CRAIG

PRAISE FOR HUMMINGBIRDS... AND OTHER STORIES

"I haven't cried like this in a while. *When The Hummingbirds Danced In A Honeysuckle Sky* is a stark examen of redemption. With unfiltered beauty, Patrick Craig draws the darkest of masculine and feminine trauma to the impossible, hoped for light of undeserved, tender, most patient love. To give, without thought of return, to sacrifice without reserve, and constancy, this is what you'll find in Craig's muscular narrative of what it means to be saved... from oneself. "

— ANN MALLEY, AUTHOR OF THE DIAMOND
DOG SERIES

"Patrick Craig has come through with another well written book. Exceptional and real characters kept me totally engrossed and emotionally invested in the story. I would definitely recommend *When The Hummingbirds Danced* to everyone! ."

— DARLENE WOOSLEY MCDOUGAL,
REVIEWER, READER

I would certainly recommend When the Hummingbirds Danced in a Honeysuckle Sky as a poignant exploration of reconciliation and legacy that is perfectly paced and powerfully told.

— K.C. FINN, FIVE STAR REVIEW — READER'S
FAVORITE

O my I loved this book. For sure is a page turner, It was a very emotional story. I believe I cried through most of it. I couldn't get the tears to quit sliding down my cheeks. Loved the characters.

— **DIANA LYNN MONTGOMERY**, DIANA'S TEA TIME REVIEWS

I have over 500 books on my Kindle, but only nine books are listed under "Favorite Christian Books". Three of those nine are the Apple Creek Dreams Series. The characters are believable, lovable, flawed human beings.

— **AMAZON READER**

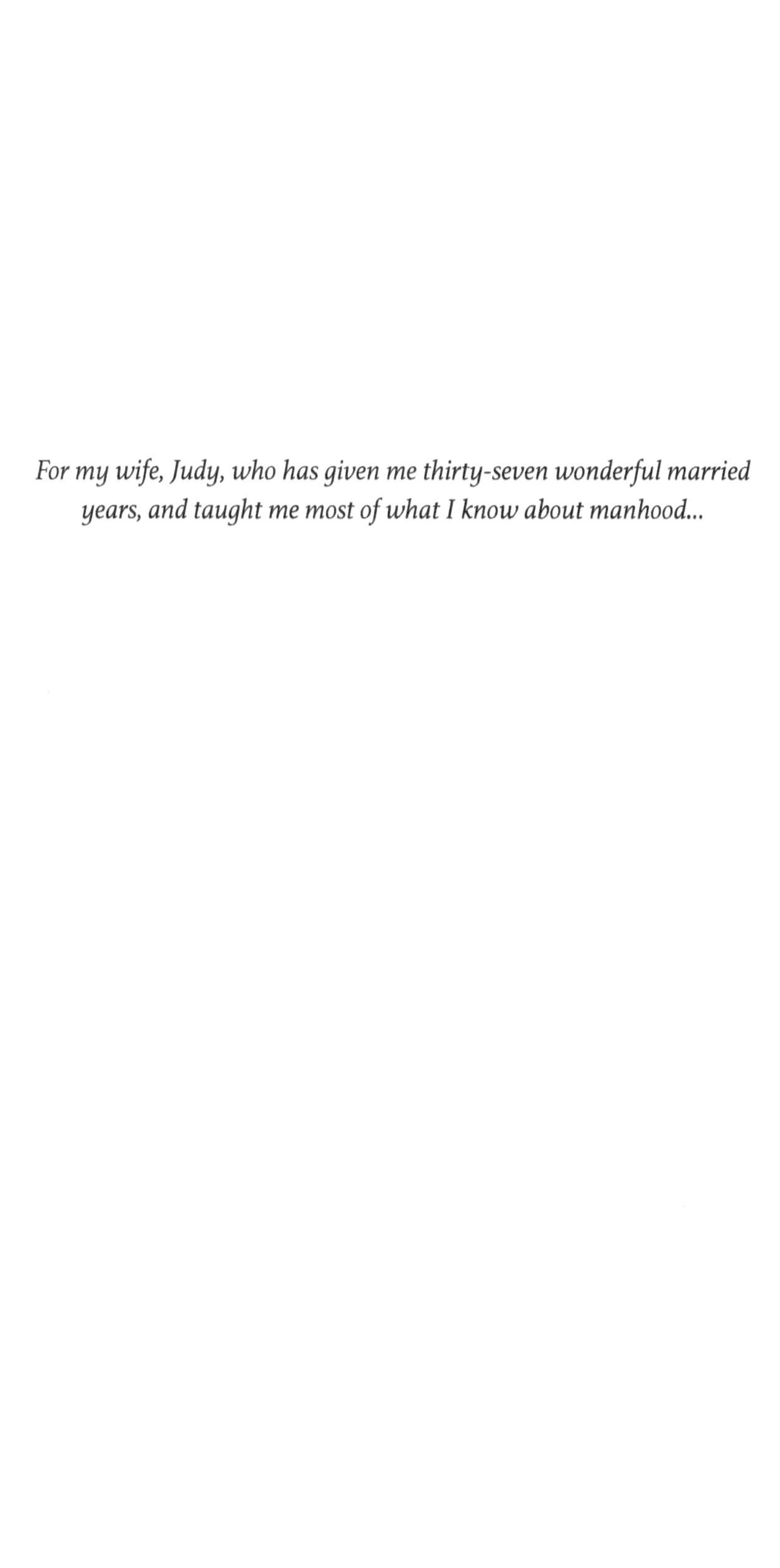

For my wife, Judy, who has given me thirty-seven wonderful married years, and taught me most of what I know about manhood...

ACKNOWLEDGMENTS

Thank you, Wes, Josie... and Margi

Cover by Cora Graphics Simona Cora Salardi

www.coragraphics.it

When The Hummingbirds Danced In A Honeysuckle Sky

Copyright © 2025 by Patrick E. Craig

Published by P&J Publishing

P.O. Box 73

Huston, Idaho 83630

Library of Congress Cataloging-in-publications Data

Craig, Patrick E., 1947-

When The Hummingbirds Danced In A Honeysuckle Sky / Patrick E. Craig

ISBN 979-8-9871451-8-0 (pbk.)

ISBN 979-8-9871451-7-3 (eBook)

Printed in the United States of America

 Created with Vellum

CONTENTS

A NOTE FROM PATRICK E. CRAIG

When The Hummingbirds Danced is a simple story about two kids who start out together on life's road and somehow lose their way. And then, years later, find it again.

I wrote it from a Christian perspective, but it is not necessarily Christian Fiction... well, in its own way it is... but I hope that those of you who are not Christian, those who might read this, will set aside any reluctance you might have if you see Christian ideas or Christian rhetoric in the interaction between Josie and Wes, and look for the archetypical themes to be found in this story—Sacrificial Love, Redemption, and Restoration.

JOSIE AND WES

Josie and Wes, Wes and Josie. Two tumbleweeds that started in the same patch, broke free, and drifted along by themselves for years and yet somehow ended up stuck fast against the same barbed-wire fence in Burns, Oregon, just after the turn of the 21st century.

Josie and Wes, my mother and father. This is their story, a story that I only uncovered after my mother died and I found letters addressed to me when I was digging through her things. She had never been one to keep notes on anything in her life, but when the "It", as she called it, came into her life, she decided she better at least let me know what she was going through. I really didn't know why then, because she abandoned me with my grandmother when I was ten, went off to be a country singer, and after that I only heard from her off and on for the next twenty years. I think I only saw her four times during all that time and she was drunk two out of the four. It was only when she found out she was sick that she contacted me, in desperation, I'm sure. She wanted me to come be with her, but I couldn't. Grandma was dead. I had my kid and was working two jobs just to feed us. That, and it's a long way from Texas to Oregon if you don't have any money.

The interesting thing is, about the time she called, I had been restarting a relationship with my dad, another ghost that I had not seen in years. Something happened to him and I guess he decided he cared about the girl he fathered, and because of that we were starting to build a tenuous relationship. When I told him about mom he responded in a way that was very surprising. And the good Lord added another chapter to the story of Josie and Wes.

I just want to make it clear, this is not really my story at all except as a postscript. What details I didn't find in her letters, my father filled in. He was with her at the end, and how that came about is a story of deep longing, utter despair and, in the end, great redemption. Because I missed being with her when she passed, I somehow feel that my role in this story is to share Josie and Wes with someone who reads this— someone who might have looked for love in all the wrong places and been seriously burned, like Josie and Wes.

And what I found as I wrote this story down is this; when you have real love, you never lose it... it is always right there to find, if you are willing to look.

He was a buckaroo cowboy with a dollar in his pocket..
She was a little-town girl with an old silver locket...

Margi

BURNS

osie Winters drove her 1973 Ford pickup into Burns, Oregon. Piled in the back and covered by a tied-down tarp, was a wide-ranging assortment of furniture, boxes, and suitcases. Attached to the ball hitch sticking out from under the rusted rear bumper was a funky white horse trailer. Inside the trailer in the front was more stuff. In the back was an old black horse.

Josie pulled up to the stoplight on the main street and looked out the driver-side window. Burns, Oregon, is not a metropolis. Neither is it a haven for philosophers, nor does it have a bronze foundry like Joseph, a little town further north in the Wallowa country—a foundry that, if Burns, Oregon, had one, might attract the artsy-fartsy crowd from Portland, tourists ready to part with their money in a myriad of day-tripper traps, art galleries, ice cream palaces and antique stores.

No, Burns, Oregon had none of that. Burns is basically a wide spot on Highway 78, about halfway between Winnemucca, Nevada and The Dalles, Oregon, as the crow flies. Burns is an eclectic assortment of museums, rock shops, and western art galleries dotting a small Main Street. If you are coming from

Reno, Nevada, like Josie, you find Burns by turning off Interstate 80 at the second Winnemucca exit, taking a left at the far end of town, driving up the endless empty miles of Highway 95 for seven hours through Orovada, and McDermitt, and turning left again at Burns Junction. You will cross into Mountain Time at the bowling pin radar station on 95 and then back into Pacific Time outside of town. Burns is a "don't blink or you'll miss it" kind of town. In fact, the Wikipedia article on Burns, Oregon, ought to include the word 'nondescript.'

In the year of our Lord, 2000, it had a population of 3,071, but by the time Josie Winters arrived, four years later, the number of people had declined by about ten percent.

Summers in Burns are short, hot, and mostly clear weather. The winters are freezing, snowy and cloudy and last from October to June, with a greater than twelve percent chance of rain or snow on any given day. This gives Burns three noticeable seasons—green, brown, and white.

Josie Winters could live with all these things. The one aspect of Burns she didn't like much was the wind. High desert is just that—high desert. The Steen mountains are off in the distance and there are not enough big trees growing in the sand and clay soil between them and town to act as windbreaks. Because of the town's situation, out on the arid eastern Oregon range, wind can be a constant companion.

Indeed, it seemed to Josie that the wind was always blowing in Burns, Oregon. Every time she had come, first to look at places, then to complete the sale, and now to settle in, the wind had been blowing. But when she thought about it, she decided she could live with the wind as well. Because it was some genus of wind—either the one blowing the dust down the main street of town, or perhaps a divine breath—that came along one day, picked her up out of her shabby little life in Reno, Nevada, and blew her north right up to Burns, Oregon. It was a strong wind, because it carried all her household goods and her horse, Salty, with her. It also brought the last of her bank account including the settlement she got from husband number three as payment for getting out of his life—just enough to buy five acres and a run-down house outside of town and live comfortably, if not meagerly.

What it didn't carry to Burns was her drunken live-in boyfriend or his two other scattered-around-Reno girlfriends. That was a good thing. But try as she might, while she was rolling up to Burns, tumbleweed fashion, she couldn't shake the rotating carousel in her head—the failures, the lies, the broken parts of her life and especially the memories. No, the wind couldn't blow the shadows of her past into the land of the lotus-eaters, but at least it got her out of Reno. Well, something did, whatever or whomever it was.

And so, one August day in 2004, she sashayed into Burns in her worn-out truck, stopped by the real estate office to get her final paper-work and title deed, and drove the flat, treeless five miles out of town to her new home.

Somewhere on the journey to her ranchette, she suddenly had a feeling she didn't recognize, and she wasn't sure she liked it. For the first time in her life, she knew she might be where she was supposed to be. It was such a strange feeling. She pulled the truck off the road, stopped, and did a quick inventory.

I'm Josie Winters. Before today, I have never been happy, well, except once, a long time ago... but I do love my horse. And somehow, I know... I will never leave this place.

Those thoughts scared her. They scared her because Josie Winters was a loser. She had never succeeded at anything or won anything, ever... except, of course, the time she took home a $2,000 jackpot from an Elko, Nevada, slot machine after a three-night gig with her CW band, a jackpot her besotted bass-player boyfriend magically turned into a very large collection of Johnny Walker Red bottles and several cases of empty Bud cans tossed into the trash dumpster outside her apartment.

Now the boyfriend was kaput, the band was no longer an

entity, and Josie, after a seven-hour drive, sat in her truck considering the possibility that this latest move might work out. A question. Would she be happy?

No, she decided, happiness was not for Josie Winters. But maybe, just maybe, she could at least find some peace in Burns, Oregon. Maybe...

SHE STARTED up the truck and headed on. The brown summer-burnt desert stretched off into a hazed nothingness. An orange sign—Open Range—reminded her to stay alert for cows on the road, and then three mailboxes with her number on the first one appeared alongside the highway. 71885. She slowed and turned left onto the gravel drive. On the right was a white house with a white fence—well-kept, purple, yellow and red flowers in a bed in front of the porch, green lawn with an impact sprinkler set in the middle sending a stream of water arcing clockwise around the grass. A nice place.

That would be the Sacks

The road turned from gravel to washboard, and the truck started shaking, so she slowed down. Another house, less well-kept, brick wainscoting along the bottom half of the front wall, tan peeling paint above that. A couple of rusty cars with weeds growing up around them, and an old John Deere tractor completed the Joad-ish scene. An old man was in the yard, white hair, cigarette, denim overhauls, unshaven, and a dirty t-shirt. He waved but didn't smile.

John Gibson. Gibson? No, Garland. John Garland.

Then she was at her driveway. 71885 in a hand-written script on a white board nailed to the fence post. She turned off the washboard onto a fairly-new asphalt drive, one of the last improvements made by the previous owner. One hundred feet more and then she pulled into a wide circle in front of the house.

In the middle of the circle was a patch of weeds with a red-hatted lawn gnome and a moss-encrusted bird bath perched in the middle. The water only came half-way up the sides of the bowl and the moss above the water-line was brown and dead.

Lotta work here.

A front porch with white posts holding up a slightly sagging roof. In between the posts were friezes of gingerbread. One or two sections had pieces broken out.

As is. Kinda like what I say when I meet a guy in a bar.

When she pulled up, she saw a basket on the porch with some packages, what looked like a card and some flowers. They were purple, yellow, and red. She got out of her truck and went back to the trailer to get Salty out. He knickered appreciatively as Josie led him down the ramp and headed him around to the slightly off-kilter barn behind the house. She pulled open the big door and stepped inside. It was dark, with little beams of light poking their fingers through several holes in the shingle roof. A pigeon flapped off a beam above the loft and several more rose flapping. She jumped. The birds settled back down. She took a breath and looked around.

The barn was cool and she could see little motes of dust floating in the beams of light. The smell was familiar—alfalfa, horse manure and dust. She was surprised to find a stall cleaned out with hay in the feeder. It was a pleasant touch after a long day on the road.

Salty was a bargain-hunter horse, one of many mustangs rounded up off the desert and broken for riding. But now he was old, an equine antique destined for the dog food factory— destined, except Josie saw an ad for an auction put on by the BLM Adopt-A-Horse program that piqued her interest. She wandered the barn where the beat-up nags were for sale and cruised the aisles of stalls until one horse put his ears up and stuck his head over the rail. Josie walked over, the horse gave her a nuzzle and that was that. She liked the horse because he reminded her of herself—aging, beat-up, too many unskilled riders, and ragged around the fetlock. She plunked down the hundred bucks and led him out to her also aging horse-trailer—an inheritance from hubby number two, a rodeo clown and all-around jerk, who looked on too much red likker one night, forgot where he was, and steered his pickup into the Truckee River.

She called the horse Salty, because when she ran him he sweated and, unless she rubbed him down right away, the sweat dried into salty patterns on his skin. She left him eating the hay contentedly and went around to the front of the house, walked up on the porch and picked up the card.

Hi, neighbor. I've left you a few "welcome to the neighborhood" snacks. I'm the first house on this road, the white one with the green barn. I knew you were bringing your horse, so I brought over some hay and put it in the stall. You can pay me later. Some milk and eggs in the frig. Your toilets are clean and I made up your bed with some of my stuff. Didn't know if you would be too tired to do it yourself. Anything else you need, just let me know.

Amanda Sacks

Josie picked up the basket. What looked like peanut butter cookies wrapped in saran wrap, a loaf of shepherd's bread, also in saran wrap, and the flowers.

Nice.

A lump formed in her throat.

Nobody does nice things for me. Wait until she gets to know me.

She got out the key.

As is. At the price they asked I couldn't afford not to buy it.

She opened the screen door. It shifted in her hand and she could see that one hinge had pulled out of the frame.

I wouldn't expect otherwise.

The key stuck in the lock for a minute and then she got it to turn and the bolt slid back with a click. The door pushed open, and she stepped inside. Drawn shades, it was dark and cool and a little musty inside.

The sharp pain in her abdomen caught her unawares. It was familiar, but unexpected today, of all days.

I guess I should go see about that. Probably acid reflux.

And then the pain came with a rush, like someone had driven a knife into her side. So intense it drove her to her knees. She gasped for breath and then the pain was so hard that she passed out.

And that is where Amanda Sacks found Josie Winters ten minutes later—sprawled across the threshold of her new home, out cold.

Chapter Two

DOCTORS

osie Winters knew nothing about medicine. She was one of those grown-up-in-America girls who went to the doctor because her mother took her, sat blush-red embarrassed, looking out the window, while the male doctor examined her after she started her monthlies, and then, for the next forty-two years, only went once a year to hear the doctor say she was good for another trip around the sun. Going to the doctor was one of those things she did, like shopping or bar-hopping or reading the newspaper—occasionally and with little thought.

Now she was sitting across the desk from Doctor Gary Sorensen. Gary was young, too young for Josie, but what could she do? The old town doctor, Doctor Phil Harris, the one she had planned on using, had retired a month before Josie arrived. Gary Sorensen had taken over his practice and Josie had fallen into line. After all, he was just a doctor.

Dr. Sorenson spread his notes and reports out on the desk in front of him. "How long have you had the pains in your stomach area?"

Josie shrugged. "I don't know, four or five months. Why?"

"I ran some blood tests after your friend brought you in last week." He paused and swallowed nervously. "I want you to see a specialist. He's in Boise. It's only about three hours from here."

Josie felt a strange knot in her chest. "Why a specialist? It's just indigestion... isn't it?"

Dr. Sorenson shook his head. "I think it may be more than that. That's why you need to see my friend. I checked and your insurance will cover the visit."

Josie shifted in her seat. "Just be honest, Doctor. What's going on with me?"

"Well, Ms. Winters..."

"Oh, for gosh' sake, my name is Josie. I haven't been Ms. Winters since I was sixteen."

"Okay... Josie. I think... I mean, your tests indicate..."

"Spit it out, Doctor. I've been around the quad a few times. I can take it."

Her words belied the sinking feeling in her gut.

The doctor sat up in his chair. "Okay then. The tests indicate pancreatic cancer. I was suspicious because of the pain. Pancreatic cancer can press on the coeliac plexus or damage it, causing pain in the tummy area and back. Nerve pain can come and go and can be difficult to describe. Some people say it feels like a burning, shooting or stabbing pain, or like pins and needles. So I ran specific tests and... that's what I think, at least with my limited test facility. HDH Clinic is not exactly Johns Hopkins." He tried to smile.

"So that's why I need the trip to Boise?"

"Yes, Dr. Fred Cranston was my teacher in medical school. He's the top in his field—Oncology, the treatment of cancer. I've contacted him and made you an appointment for next week, on Thursday."

"That might be difficult, Doctor. I will have to arrange transportation and a place to stay. I don't think my truck will make it there and back."

"Well, you have a week. Maybe you can find someone to take you. He will only need a few hours, I'm sure. If you leave here early, say around 7:00 a.m., you can be there by 10:00. He's cleared his schedule after 11:00 that morning as a favor to me. You could be back that evening."

Josie got up. "Okay, Doctor, I'll try to get something arranged. I'll call you." She pivoted and walked out. He did not see the tears in her eyes or her trembling hands.

JOSIE WINTERS SAT at the table in her kitchen. She had just gotten off the phone with Dr. Cranston. Now... everything had changed.

"Ms. Winters? Doctor Cranston. I'm calling about your tests. I... I'm afraid Gary was right. It is pancreatic cancer, and it's stage four."

Josie felt her skin go clammy.

"What does that mean?"

"Barring a miracle of some sort, it's terminal."

A long silence.

"How... how long do I have, Doctor?"

"Five months, six at the most."

"And there is nothing I can do? Chemo? Radiation?"

"No, I'm afraid not. It's very aggressive, and it's metastasized."

"What does that mean?"

"It means the cancer has spread and is inoperable. It's too late for chemotherapy."

"What about the pain?"

"You need to start with a non-opioid—aspirin or acetaminophen at first. As time goes by, you will need something stronger, codeine or morphine. I can prescribe it for you."

"But isn't that addicting?" Josie realized what a stupid question that was.

"Well, if you take oral morphine on a timed schedule you can avoid that, but, in the long run, I'm afraid it won't matter. I'm sorry to be so blunt, but that's where we stand."

Another long silence. The doctor spoke up.

"I am sorry about this, Ms. Winters, but you need to hear it as it is. Do you have someone who could help you? A friend... family?"

"I guess I could call my daughter. She's in Texas."

But we haven't spoken for ten years.

"Well, I think it's time for you to put your affairs in order."

"Hello?"

The voice sounded tinny and distant, but Josie felt a pang of remembrance. Margarita. Wesley had named her after his favorite drink. Margi never knew she was a joke to her dad. Josie remembered her daughter when she was little. There were some good times, mostly when Wesley was off on the rodeo circuit.

"Hello?" The voice came again.

"Margarita... it's your mom."

There was a silence. It was a silence born of years of neglect and forgotten birthdays, and all the baggage of Josie's own broken dreams. She heard Margi sigh.

"What do you want, Mom? And how did you get my number?"

How did we get here? She's my daughter.

"I called my cousin, Beth. She knew where you were. I know we haven't spoken in a while, but I was hoping..."

"A while? That's funny. And hoping what, Mom? You want to get together? Be friends? Take me shopping?"

"Margi, don't...please. Let me say what I have to say and then you can beat me up if you want to."

Nothing for a moment. "Okay, what?"

"I'm sick, Margi. Real sick."

"What are you saying, Mom?"

"I just got a call from my doctor. I have pancreatic cancer."

"What do you mean?"

"Just what I said, Margi, I have stage four pancreatic cancer."

It was the first time Josie had said the words. It was almost like vomiting.

"Stage four? That's bad isn't it?"

Josie took a deep breath. "He says I have about six months left."

Margarita's voice softened. "What are you going to do?"

Josie shook her head.

What am I going to do?

"I don't know, Margi. But I thought I should tell you."

The hardness came back. "That's just great, Mom, just great. You take off with that band, dump me with Grandma and I see you four times in twenty years. Then, out of the blue, you call just to let me know you're dying? After years of nothing, no letters, no calls, not even a kiss my behind. Unbelievable. Just unbelievable."

Josie's hands were trembling. "I know, I know. I was messed up, honey. I didn't know what I was doing."

"And that's supposed to let you off the hook?"

"I was hoping maybe you could come and see me."

Margarita laughed, only it wasn't a laugh. "I'm a thirty-two-year-old single mom with a five-year-old boy. I work two shifts a day at a crummy restaurant just to make ends meet. I don't even have a car. I'm lucky I have a place to live, and I wouldn't if Gram hadn't left her house to me. And you want me to come see you? Give me one, just one, good reason."

Another longer silence, crushed dreams, roads that went nowhere.

"I just thought..."

"I'm sorry for you, Mom, I really am. It's bad luck. But I can't come."

Josie could taste the distance between them.

Then quieter. "Have you told Dad?"

"Wes?" It was Josie's turn to laugh. "Wes has been gone a long time, Josie. Thirty-eight years. I don't even know where he is. Besides, what could Wes do?"

"I don't know, Mom. I really don't. But you should at least tell him."

"That's a lose-lose proposition, Margi. Your father is a drunk, and he never did anything for anybody but himself."

"People can change, Mom. I've been talking to Dad lately and, well, he's different."

"You don't seem to believe that about me. I've changed too."

"That's why you haven't called me in ten years? At least he did."

Josie sighed and thought about that. "To be honest, Margi, I didn't know what to say. I wanted to call, and then I didn't and a year went by and then it was ten, but I'm calling now."

"Sure, when you need something. How about when I needed something? A mom to tell me I was beautiful when I went to the prom, or give me advice so I wouldn't get pregnant when I was seventeen and then abort my baby, someone to tell me not to live with the jerk who fathered Billy..."

The tears on her face surprised Josie. "I'm sorry, Margi."

Her voice was so quiet she almost didn't hear herself.

"What?"

Louder. "I said, I'm sorry, Margi. Sorry for everything. Sorry for you, sorry for Billy, sorry for my messed-up life, sorry I'm going to die before I can make it up to you, just sorry."

Josie started to hang up. She heard Margarita say something, so she put the phone back to her ear.

"What, Margi?"

"Do you still live in Reno?"

"No, I moved. I'm in Burns, Oregon."

"Burns, Oregon? Where the heck is that?"

"It's about three hours west of Boise, Idaho."

"Is there an airport?"

"Yeah, a little one. I think you can fly into Boise and catch a local flight over to Burns Municipal."

"When did you move there?"

Josie shook her head. "About a week ago. I thought this was going to be a safe place for me. When I was driving here, I had the strangest feeling I would never leave here. I was right."

Another silence. Another sigh. "Okay, Mom. I'll try to come and see you. I can't promise anything, but I'll see."

The phone went dead.

Josie stared at the phone in her hand. Something welled up in her, like heartburn, or a poorly chewed potato stuck in her throat. She hung it up, leaned against the wall and then slid down to the floor and wept. She sat there for a long time.

Finally, she got up and went to the sink. She ran the water until it was ice cold and then she put her head under the faucet. The shock of the water was like a blow to the back of the head, but it cleared her thoughts. She stayed there for a long time and then reached up and turned off the faucet. There was a red checked dish towel hanging over the stove handle. She grabbed it and wrapped it around her head. Icy-cold water ran out from under the edge and down her face. She stood there at the sink for a long time, the sleeves and neck of her sweatshirt soaking up the water.

Then she walked through the kitchen and went into her bedroom. A pile of bath towels lay on the bed where she had unpacked. She picked one off the top of the pile and went into the bathroom. Stripping off her wet clothes, she turned the shower on. When the water was steaming, she stepped in.

I can count the number of times I will stand in a hot shower. I know how many more times I will ride Salty. I can plan all my meals for the rest of my life.

When she got out of the shower, she put on dry clothes and

went outside. The sun was sinking in the West behind a low range of hills. The desert was dry and the grass that had been verdant in the Spring was now brown, dry, scraggly like a three-day beard that stretched to the horizon. She walked out to the fence that separated her place from the BLM land. There was a green metal pasture gate hung between two rock cairns, fastened with a length of chain. She opened it and walked out onto the prairie.

If I just keep walking, I can walk into those hills and just lay down somewhere.

She took a few more steps.

So, this is it. I will die alone, like I've lived.

She stared at the sinking sun. It was slipping piece by piece into the crack where tomorrow lives.

But I have no tomorrow...

Chapter Three

FRIENDS

The next morning Josie walked down the gravel driveway to where the Sack's property started and the shared driveway turned to asphalt. It was one full week since she got the news about the "It" as she called it. The "It" had taken on a life of its own. It was her constant companion. It tweaked her good from time to time. It even lived in her dreams. The net result was a layer of depression she had not felt since Wes left her almost forty years before.

This is not good.

She turned her steps into Amanda's driveway and her spirits lifted a bit. Amanda was becoming a friend—not a good friend in Josie's thinking because she shied from calling any relationship good—but... maybe a 'friend' friend.

Amanda was diplomatic, no-nonsense, and didn't make a big deal over the "It." It was as though Amanda saw life for what it is —a circle of days that last as long as they do, and then they are over. It is what it is, they are what they are. She had a gruff way of talking that belied a tender heart. Somehow, that appealed to Josie.

Amanda's husband, Ben, was a rancher. That's what people in

Burns called anyone with over ten acres and two horses. Josie had aspired to rancher-hood when she moved to Burns, but all dreams were put away. A rancher Josie would never be.

Amanda waved from behind the kitchen window and made motions like drinking from a cup.

Yeah, coffee works.

It was Wednesday, September 1, 2004. She had listened to the radio this morning. A bunch of terrorists had taken over a school in Russia and were holding over a thousand people hostage, including hundreds of school kids. Johnny Bragg, the doo-wop singer, had died, and a court in Colorado had dropped rape charges against Kobe Bryant, the basketball player.

Wonder how much that cost?

The town of Burns was gearing up for Labor Day, which was happening on Monday. Lots of tourists came through on the way to the coast, the mountains, or Bend, or Wallowa Lake. The town made a determined effort to snag some of them as they passed with events like the Burns, Oregon, Labor Day Festival, or the Old-Time Fiddlers. There was also The Harney County Fair and assorted picnics. Josie grinned to herself.

Desperation reigns supreme in Burns, Oregon... I should know.

As she walked up to the front door, Amanda opened it and motioned Josie to head around the house.

"Come on to the barn. I want to show you something."

Josie walked around, and Amanda came out with two cups of coffee. Amanda's was black, but Josie's was light-colored from the half and half. Amanda knew that about her already, which was one reason Josie categorized their friendship as "getting there."

They headed across the backyard, through a gate and into the barn.

"How are you today, Josie?"

"Middlin'." It was an expression she learned from her second husband, the rodeo clown from Arkansas. It meant "middlin'."

Amanda led her through the semi-dark of the barn and over

to a stall against the back wall. She leaned over the stall door and pointed to the back corner. Curled up in a small heap of hay was a small calico cat. Nestled up against her, nursing, were four tiny kittens. Josie's heart took a turn. She loved cats.

"Brand new last night. Wanna see'em?"

Josie nodded. "Oh, yes."

"Thought so." Amanda put her cup on the post, swung the stall door open and Josie went in. She knelt beside the little momma and set her cup down gently. The calico looked up and gave a quiet 'meow.' The four tiny babies piled together at momma's breasts, making little mewling sounds as they nursed and pushed their tiny feet against her. Josie looked at them. Two orange, one calico and a black one with white socks on all four little paws. Josie pointed.

"Can I have that one?"

Amanda grinned. "Figured so. Already tagged him for you."

Josie looked up at her neighbor. She tried a smile. It came out crooked.

I've only known you for ten days. You don't know me at all. There's no way you could ever like me. Bad to the bone, that's Josie Winters.

"Give them two weeks and we will see if they are ready to wean."

Josie looked down at the kitten.

Two weeks. That leaves 5 months and two weeks max.

"You know what? I better pass. By the time he gets weaned, I will only have a few months left."

Amanda put her arm around Josie's shoulder. "You should take him. He'll be okay when you're... when you... Oh, honey, I'm sorry." Amanda began to cry.

Josie looked at Amanda in surprise. And then pulled her close and started to cry, too.

"No one has ever cried for me, Amanda."

They stood there for a long time in the half-dark.

Labor Day in Burns, Oregon. Josie watched the cars stream down Main Street in both directions. She was sitting in the passenger seat of Amanda's white Ford 250. They were making their way slowly through the traffic. People walked down the sidewalks, flags were flying from light poles, an occasional revved up motorcycle wove in and out through the cars and trucks. It felt small, rural, homey, but somehow, frail.

Not much like Reno, but that's a good thing.

"Honey, I need to stop at Tack and Feed. You need anything? We can throw it in the back."

Josie nodded. "I need a couple of bales of alfalfa for Salty. He's getting old, and he's protein deficient."

Like me.

Amanda pulled the truck into a space out front of the tack store and they got out. Together, they walked into the establishment.

"Howdy ladies." A tall man came around the counter and shook Amanda's hand. "And this is...?"

"My new neighbor, Josie. Josie, this is Bert Franklin. He owns this rat trap."

Bert grinned. "How's Ben?"

Amanda shrugged. "I keep trying to get him to slow down, but you know him, Bert. Go, go, go."

"Aw, Ben will never stop buckin' bales. He can't."

"Speaking of bales, Bert, can you get Josie a couple? Throw them in my pickup."

"Sure thing, Amanda."

"Hey, want to go get a burger at the Silver Mine?"

Josie nodded. "That sounds good."

They went back out to the truck. Bert was just bucking the second bale into the back. He stepped up close to Josie. "Hey, want to go get a beer sometime?"

Josie looked at Bert. A good-lookin' tall glass of water, but she could smell the rodeo on him. "Thanks for the invite, Bert, but I don't have the time."

"Aw, come on, there's not that much to do in Burns."

Amanda pushed between them. "Bert, when she says she ain't got time, she means just that. Let's go, girlfriend. My stomach's so empty it feels like my throat got slit."

Josie had heard that one before, but she appreciated Amanda running a screen for her. They headed downtown. In a few minutes, they pulled into a parking place in front of The Silver Mine. Local brewery, restaurant, and live music venue. Josie knew the deal. As they climbed out, she saw guys carrying equipment out of a van. A Twin Reverb amp, a couple of guitar cases, a pedal steel in its case, assorted drums.

"Man, I wish I had a nickel for every piece of equipment I've carried into a bar."

Amanda stopped. "You were in a band?"

Josie shrugged. "A few."

"Oh, honey, that's cool. What did you play?"

"I played some guitar, but mostly I was the lead singer."

Amanda shook her head. "You know somebody long enough to think you know everything about them..."

They both laughed. Josie was going through the door when she ran into a guy who was obviously coming back out for more stuff. "S'cuse me." He went past and then turned and looked again. "Josie?"

Josie looked back.

Now there's a face I thought I'd never see again.

"Tommy? Tommy Franklin?"

"Josie, for goodness' sake. What in the world are you doing here?"

"I live in Burns now. Got a mini-ranchette outside town. The question should be, what are you doing here?"

Tommy grinned. "How the mighty have fallen, eh?"

Josie shook her head. "The last time I saw you, you were on the way to Nashville. Gonna sign a recording contract or sell some songs or..."

"Yeah, well, the best laid plans of mice and men." Tommy put down the guitar case he was holding and stepped up. "I know we didn't part on the best of terms, Josie, and I'm sorry." He held out his arms.

Josie hesitated for a moment. "Okay, Tommy." She stepped over and gave him a hug. Not a big hug but a 'I can forgive but I won't forget' hug. Then she nodded at Amanda, who was standing by with a kind of dopey, groupie grin on her face. "Amanda, meet Tommy Franklin, the world's greatest guitar player. And if you don't believe me, just ask him." She smiled to soften the blow.

"Aw, Josie, I said I was sorry." He shook Amanda's hand.

Josie looked at the other guys still hauling equipment into the club. "From all the roadie activity, I assume you are playing here—a far cry from Nashville, indeed. What happened?"

Tommy looked at his feet. "Couldn't stop looking on the booze. I found out that the guys in Nashville are deadly serious about their business. Took me a year to discover that the wannabes and the movers and shakers live in two separate worlds. The successful folks are mostly clean and sober. A lesson learned too late, I'm afraid."

Josie patted him on the shoulder. "So, I take it nobody recorded my song?"

Tommy turned red and stammered. "Josie, I swear I gave you credit every time I showed it to somebody. I would have split any royalties with you."

"Split, Tommy? My words, Wes's music, your guitar part? Doesn't seem like that earned you a split. More like ninety/ten, if we did your arrangement. But I guess it's smoke in the wind now. You copyrighted my song when I was too dumb to know what was going on. Maybe you'll give it back someday... if I'm still around."

"What do you mean?"

"Nothin', Tommy, just nothin'." She turned to Amanda. "I'm not hungry for a burger any more. Isn't there someplace we can get some fish and chips?"

"Aw, Josie, don't go. How many times do I have to say I'm sorry? It was a long time ago and yes, I was a drunk and a punk and I ripped you off. But I paid the price." He pointed up at the sign over the door. *Tommy Franklin and his Rollin' Tumbleweeds.* "As you can see. How the mighty have fallen."

Suddenly Josie realized that none of it mattered. Tommy, her music, her old life—it was all just a dream—a bad dream that was ending soon. What was that speech from Shakespeare? The one she learned in school? Oh yeah, Macbeth...

Tomorrow, and tomorrow, and tomorrow,
Creeps in this petty pace from day to day,
To the last syllable of recorded time;
And all our yesterdays have lighted fools
The way to dusty death.
Out, out, brief candle!
Life's but a walking shadow, a poor player,
That struts and frets his hour upon the stage,
And then is heard no more. It is a tale
Told by an idiot, full of sound and fury,
Signifying nothing...

YEAH, out, out brief candle.

"Josie, Josie...?"

Josie looked at Tommy. He took his hat off and held it in front of him. "Why don't you come back tonight and sit in? I taught the fellas some of the old tunes. Please, Josie, for *auld lang syne*?" Tommy smiled his best infectious grin.

Josie stared at Tommy for a long time. She reached back and scratched her neck. "I'll think about it. When's your set?"

"Nine o'clock. Please, Josie. It will be good to hear you sing again."

"Like I said, I'll think about it. Come on, Amanda." Josie turned and walked back to the truck.

Not a lot of time. Let bygones be bygones, Josie.

Chapter Four

SAME OLD SONG

*S*eptember eighth was not a good day. The pain had come early, without warning and without mercy. Josie lay in bed close to tears. The sun was coming up in the East, but it was dragging grey clouds and an icy wind with it. She could hear the glass in the windows rattle and a mournful moaning sound seemed to rush by outside, like Valkyries on patrol. Josie waited for as long as she could and then got up and went into the bathroom. The Ibuprofen was no longer knocking the pain.

Doctor Gary laid it out for her in his office during her last visit. "Common medicines used for cancer pain include opioids or narcotics, acetaminophen and non-steroidal anti-inflammatory drugs. We should start you on Ibuprofen and then move up as the pain increases."

"Increases? I don't like the sound of that, Doctor. The current level is pretty much kickin' my tail."

Doctor Gary frowned. "I can't say it any other way. Pain is an ever-present companion with this type of cancer. Once the acetaminophen stops working, we can move you to a long-acting oral morphine or other opioids. If you can't take opioids orally, we can give you a continuous-release medication skin patch or medication suppositories."

Josie grinned. "I can't un-see that last one, Doc."

Doctor Gary smiled too, then his frown came back. "I'm really sorry, Josie, I really am. I'm a little in over my head with this—brand new practice, hoping to fix up broken legs and maybe an occasional bull gore."

"Instead, you get me."

"Yeah, I got you and the problem is, I really like you. I know that doesn't sound professional, but this is Burns and I used to think that family medicine meant your patients were like family. I guess I just got too invested. I'll try to be..."

Josie interrupted. "No, Doctor Gary. I appreciate very much that you care—that you treat this like a profession instead of a business. I never trusted doctors, never knew much about them, but I guess if I had a doctor...," she smiled... "which I do..., I would want them to care like you do. It helps, it really does."

Gary looked out the window for a minute, then turned back. "Okay, good, that's that then."

Josie pushed on to spare him any more discomfort. "So, morphine after the Ibuprofen?"

"Yes. But here's what I know. Even though I know you are worried about getting hooked..."

"Not worried, Doc, scared to death. I was a musician, remember. I worked in a town where drugs, especially opioids like OxyContin, were as available as M&Ms. I watched friends just disappear. So that's why."

"Josie, if you take the medication as a daily regimen instead of just when you have pain, it will work better and your system will assimilate it better. Addiction becomes less of an option."

Josie left the office a little less nervous, with a prescription for an oral morphine. She vowed to take it as little as possible, but now she stood in front of her bathroom mirror, looking at the pain etched on her face. She sighed, reached in to the cabinet, and took out the jar.

Take one every five hours for pain. Okay. That which I feared most has come upon me.

It RAINED THAT AFTERNOON. The icy wind and grey clouds bore fruit in large, splattering drops, starting about three o'clock. About four, she heard Amanda's ATV pull up in front. She went in and started the coffee she had never gotten around to. She knew it was the morphine.

I have to keep focused. I can't just sit here staring at the walls.

The doorbell rang, and she went. Amanda stood there, but she did not look happy. Josie ushered her into the front room.

"Coffee?"

Amanda nodded. She seemed distracted.

Josie went and fetched the coffee and then handed Amanda hers. "What's up, Amanda? You look worried."

"I am. Ben got up this morning, and he was acting weird. He was slurring his words and he couldn't remember some things he was going to do today."

"Did you take him to Gary?"

"Yeah. Not good. Gary thinks he had a mini-stroke. I kept telling him he needed to take it easy. But he just never quits."

"What does that mean?"

"Gary says he's got to rest, and slow down. I've got to babysit him more and watch him for signs of any more strokes."

"Well..., yeah."

"That just means I can't spend time with you as much."

There was silence and then it came clear to Josie and it was like a drink of clean water.

She's been hospicing me, care-taking.

Josie went over and sat down on the couch next to Amanda

and put her arms around her. She spoke to her quietly. "Amanda, I love that you care enough to look after me, but Ben's your husband. Take care of him now, spend more time. He's going to be in the house more and you must watch over him until he gets well. If he needs to do any exercises or stuff like that, help him."

Amanda looked at Josie. "I know. It's just that I really felt…"

"What?"

"Promise you won't think I'm a nut job?"

"I promise."

Amanda took a deep breath. "I was sure that the Lord told me to take care of you."

"What?"

"You promised."

Josie looked at Amanda. "You mean the Lord as in… God?"

Amanda nodded. "The first day you got here, when you passed out in the doorway, I was sure God spoke to me and told me to take care of you."

"You mean, you heard an audible voice?"

Amanda shook her head. "No, it was just… like… an impression I got."

Josie wanted to phrase her next question carefully. "So… are you… a Christian?"

Amanda nodded again. "Yes."

And then Josie felt a little heat growing in her. She didn't much like Christians. "Okaayy, that's interesting. I wondered why you seemed so attentive. Am I your 'field white for harvest' or something?"

Amanda went pale. "I should have kept my mouth shut."

Josie stood up. "Look, Amanda, I'm not a Christian and every Christian I have ever dealt with always had an angle. They wanted to get me saved, or get me to join their church, or get my money…" The memory came back. "Or worse."

"I don't want any of those things. I just want to be your friend and help you."

Josie walked to the front door. "I don't do friends very well. I don't trust people, because they have always burned me. Besides, you don't know me. I'm rotten to the core. I'm not a nice person. I was married three times and every one of my husbands found someone better to play around with. I am not worth much and if there is a God, which I sincerely doubt, He has dealt me a dirty deal my whole life. You don't need a friend like me."

"Josie, I…"

"You know, Amanda, it seems like the timing for Ben's stroke is just right. He needs you and I don't. So, let's just leave it at that. I'll be okay. I don't need anybody's help."

Josie opened the door. Amanda stood up. "Josie, you got it all wrong. I really want to be your friend."

"It's okay, Amanda. You should go home now."

Anguish crossed Amanda's face and then she went to the door. "If you change your mind, I'm just down the road."

She went out and Josie closed the door behind her.

Another one bites the dust.

AFTER AMANDA LEFT, Josie sat for a long time. The rain stopped and a washed-out sun pushed through the grey sky. Josie sighed, got up, and went out to the barn to feed Salty. When she came in, he lifted his head and snorted. He was growing his shaggy winter coat and looked fat. Josie went in the stall with a couple of alfalfa leaves and dropped them in his manger. Salty nuzzled up and pushed at her back. Josie turned and put her arms around his neck.

"Who will take care of you when I'm gone, Salty? I got nobody, so you got nobody. It always turns out this way. Josie Winters, unlovable, unapproachable, dying, soon to be dead Josie Winters. Maybe you'll die on the same day I do and I can ride you into heaven." She thought about that. "Not an option. I'm not even wanted there. If we get there, I guess I'll just hand you over to the guy at the gate and go my way."

Salty nickered and then pushed past to get the feed. Josie had a thought.

Maybe I'll go in and see Tommy play. Have a few beers, a few laughs. Get my head out of the garbage pail.

She brightened. Tommy would probably come on to her, but she knew all his moves well enough to put him in his place. You learned all the pickup lines and all the snappy comebacks when you sang in a Country and Western band, especially with Tommy Franklin.

Yeah. I just got to get out more.

———

THE SILVER MINE SMELLED LIKE, sounded like, and even tasted like every funky bar Josie had ever been in. The band was loud, the chatter and noise louder, and stale cigarette smoke permeated everything. Josie avoided the bar, which was always raunchy cowboy territory, and headed for a table in the back. The pert waitress in her line-dance jeans sashayed by and Josie ordered a Corona with a slice of lime. The band was surprisingly competent and, of course, Tommy was always good. They played a couple of songs and then Tommy did his famous Roy Clark version of 'Ghost Riders in the Sky,' which got the place hopping. After that Tommy did one called, 'You know You're in Trouble When the Bartender Cries.' It was good, very good, and Tommy put just the right pathos in his voice. They finished the set with one more partner dance tune and took a break.

Tommy came off the stage and headed toward the bar. A young gal stepped in front of him and smiled. Josie grinned. Tommy Franklin was hitting sixty-five, but he was still handsome and, well, he was in the band. Surprisingly, he brushed by her and went past the bar into the dressing room. He was back in a few minutes. This time, he came straight over to Josie's table.

"Hey, Josie. I saw you come in. Decided to do a little slumming?"

"The walls were closing in, Tommy. I just needed to get out."

"Can I sit?"

"It's a free country."

Tommy pulled up a chair. "Still drinking Corona, I see."

"I like the lime."

"Do you want to sing a couple next set?"

Josie looked at Tommy's expectant face.

A lot of water under that bridge.

"I don't know, Tommy. I haven't sung for over a year. I probably sound like a mule brayin' in a tin barn at midnight."

"Hey, Josie. If you got it, you got it. Like riding a bike."

Josie remembered. The lights, the music, the only time anybody ever liked her.

Maybe I need to feel that again.

She took a sip and let him twist. "Okay, Tommy, but just a couple."

"Will you sing 'Hummingbirds?'"

A sharp pang but not the "It."

"I guess."

"I went back and got the chart for the bass player and the pedal steel guy. They're good, they can pick it right up."

"Okay."

Tommy stood up. "Come on, it's time." They headed for the stage. The rest of the band followed. "Guys, this is Josie Winters. An old friend."

Josie looked at Tommy.

Now you're stretching it, Franklin.

A man walked up on the stage and took the mic. "Ladies and gentlemen, welcome to the Silver Mine. Tonight, for your listening and dancing pleasure, Tommy Franklin and His Rolling

Tumbleweeds." The announcer turned. "Who's the little lady?" he whispered.

"Josie Winters."

The guy turned back to the mike. "Featuring Josie Winters." He stretched it out, and the audience gave a weak response.

Tommy handed the charts to his band and then stepped to the mike. "Here's an old one by Loretta Lynn. Sing it Josie."

The band started up and Josie felt herself swing into the song. Surprisingly, it was easy, like Tommy said.

You've come to tell me something you say I ought to know
That he don't love me anymore and I'll have to let him go
You say you're gonna take him oh but I don't think you can
'Cause you ain't woman enough to take my man

SHE SANG THE SECOND VERSE. The break came, and the pedal steel swung right in.

He's good!

Josie went through the verses. There was a nice guitar break from Tommy, and then they finished up with one more chorus. The audience broke into surprised applause.

Tommy looked at Josie. "Let's do 'Fancy.'"

Josie nodded. The band broke into the opening chords of the old Reba song. Their cohesion surprised Josie. The drummer swung it. Tommy joined in on the chorus harmony and the band guys contributed the backups. When they finished, the audience had moved off the dance floor and was up against the stage, watching and whooping.

Tommy stepped up. "We'd like to do an original written by Josie and another old pal, Wes Branson. It's called, 'When The Hummingbirds Danced In A Honeysuckle Sky.'" He gave a few instructions to the band and then nodded to the pedal steel guy who picked up the intro like he had written it. Josie stepped to the Mike. She hadn't expected the flood of emotions that almost overwhelmed her. They came right through and into the song.

> *When the hummingbirds danced in a honeysuckle sky*
> *And the stars fell down on the fourth of July*
> *She never knew about love 'til she saw it in his eyes*
> *When the hummingbirds danced in a honeysuckle sky*

He was a buckaroo cowboy with a dollar in his pocket,
> *She was a little-town girl with an old silver locket.*
> *He told her that he loved her and they talked all night*
> *and all her dreams came true when he held her so tight*

When the hummingbirds danced in a honeysuckle sky
> *And the stars fell down on the fourth of July*
> *She never knew about love 'til she saw it in his eyes*
> *When the hummingbirds danced in a honeysuckle sky*

There's nothing like love when it comes like a twister
> *She was so sweet well he couldn't resist her*
> *A man makes a promise, and a woman says yes*
> *now she's a wife named Josie with a hubby called Wes*

When the hummingbirds danced in a honeysuckle sky
> *And the stars fell down on the fourth of July*
> *She never knew about love 'til she saw it in his eyes*
> *When the hummingbirds danced in a honeysuckle sky*

Sweet dreams and colors in the sky,
> *will you still be with me when the hummingbirds fly?*

I'm counting on you baby, 'cause I can't let go
Just keep on lovin' me, please keep loving me,
Tell me that you love me, and we'll never say goodbye...

WHEN THE HUMMINGBIRDS *danced in a honeysuckle sky*
    And the stars fell down on the fourth of July
    She never knew about love 'til she saw it in his eyes
    When the hummingbirds danced in a honeysuckle sky

THE SONG ENDED with the pedal steel flourish and the audience stood stunned for just a moment. Then the place went wild. Tommy looked over at Josie and nodded. But Josie was already gone.

JOSIE DROVE HOME in the dark, the lights from her truck picking up the few white pasture fences along the road. It was hard to see because of the tears in her eyes.

That song! Why did I ever fall for that sweet-talkin'...

As she pulled into her driveway, she was surprised to see a rig pulled up in front of the house. A fairly new Ford truck with an older Airstream trailer hitched on. She pulled up behind it and got out. She saw the shadow coming around the trailer toward her. A tall man with a western hat.

"Lose your way, Mister?"

The man stepped into the light and a shock went through Josie.

Wes! Wes Branson!

"Howdy, Josie. Been a long time."

Chapter Five

WES

Josie Winters stared at the man standing in the glow of her headlights. Wesley James Branson, her first husband, father of her child, a man she hated almost as much as she hated the "It."

"Wes Branson, what in the holy mother-of-pearl are you doing here?"

"Hi, Josie. Good to see you, too."

"No. I'm not kidding around. What are you doing here?" She was almost shouting.

Wes took off his hat and stepped out of the lights, so that he was standing in front of her. He held his hat in both his hands and looked down.

"I heard you were sick, and I came to help," he said quietly.

"Who told you I was sick?"

"Margarita."

"Margarita called you?"

Wes nodded. "Yeah, we've been in touch for a while now. Trying to work it out between us."

"Does she know you named her after your favorite booze?"

"Yeah." Wes looked away and then back. "I told her."

"Yeah, well, good for you. Came clean, huh?"

"I've made some changes, Josie."

"Yeah, right. Tell it to somebody who doesn't know you."

Josie stared at her ex-husband. Still tall, broad shoulders, narrow hips. A rodeo cowboy's bowed legs, big hands, hands that could be gentle... She felt her face flush. She looked away so he wouldn't see, gathered herself, looked back. The new thing was the small neat mustache that covered what looked like a scar over his lip.

"Where'd you get the scar? Bar fight?"

Wes just looked at her. Josie stared back. Finally, she spoke.

"Wes Branson, I don't know where you came from or how long it took you to get here, but you are the very last person on God's green earth that I want to see, not to mention accept anything from."

"Josie, I..."

"I don't need help. You're the second person I've said that to today, and I mean it. I don't need help."

"Do you have a lot of pain yet?"

"What?"

"Do you have a lot of pain yet?"

"What's that to you?"

"People with pancreatic cancer have pain. As you get toward the end, it puts you down. You need someone there."

"I don't have any pain."

"Your eyes say different."

"Okay, so I have pain. I still don't need help."

"You will."

"Look, Wes, just go. I don't want you here. Get in your car..."

And then the "It" bit. Hard. So hard, it took Josie to one knee. She almost screamed, but he was there. She couldn't let him see. And then he was picking her up and carrying her.

"Is the house open?"

She fumbled in her coat for the key and gave it to him. The

pain was hard and bitter, vengeful. He opened the door and carried her through.

Like he did when we were married.

"Where's your room?"

She lifted her arm, pointed.

He was so strong. Like she weighed nothing. He carried her into the room and laid her gently on the bed.

"You got any pills?"

She nodded, pointed to the bathroom door. He went in, the light came on. Josie heard the click of the cabinet and then Wes was back. "Glass? Water?"

"In the kitchen," she choked it out.

He was back in a minute. She took one pill, swallowed it with the water. He laid her back. Looked around the room. There was a blanket on the small couch by the window. He pulled it off and brought it. He covered her and tucked her in. Then he went and sat on the couch. In a few minutes the morphine kicked in and she settled. The ache was still there, but the sword thrust through the groin was gone. He said nothing, waiting.

"I'm better, Wes."

"Good. Can you get undressed?"

"Not with you here."

"I didn't mean that. Can you get yourself ready for bed?"

She nodded.

"Pajamas?"

"In the third drawer down."

He got the flannels, brought them to her.

"I'll be outside if you need me."

He started to leave. Suddenly, Josie was afraid.

"Wes?"

He stopped. "Yeah?"

"Don't leave tonight. You can park the trailer by the barn. There's a faucet you can get water out of. And there's a toilet in a room in the back of the barn. Don't leave until tomorrow, okay?"

"Whatever you want, Josie."

He walked out.

She had forgotten how he filled a doorway.

BACON. *I'm dreaming about bacon...*

Josie opened her eyes. She wasn't dreaming. The smell of cooking bacon slipped under the door. Outside, the gray had vanished, and the sun was out. A sound came through the door, a tune.

Tumblin' Tumbleweeds. Wes is whistling...

That had always been one thing she loved about Wes. When he was occupied, he started whistling. He...

Wait a minute. I don't love anything about Wes Branson. Nothing.

There was a knock on the door.

"Are you decent?"

"I'm still in bed. What do you want?"

"Thought you might like some bacon, eggs, and pancakes. Some coffee?"

Josie wanted nothing from Wes, but she was hungry, and it smelled good.

"Give me a minute." She slipped out of bed, went to the closet, and pulled out her bathrobe. She started to go out and then she turned and went into the bathroom.

I should at least look presentable.

She ran a brush through her hair and looked at her reflection in the mirror. She had new lines, some just age, but some from the pain. She was still pretty, though, what a younger man might call 'a right handsome woman.' She slipped her feet into her slippers and went to the door.

I should just tell him to leave without seeing him.

But she didn't. She went out into the kitchen. Wes had eggs in the pan, a stack of steaming pancakes on the table and a plate with a paper towel to catch the bacon grease from the strips laid out on it.

"Sit down. Coffee's hot."

She sat, and he brought her a plate with two eggs. Over medium, two strips of slightly burned bacon.

He remembered.

"Aren't you gonna eat?"

Wes shook his head. "I had my breakfast in the trailer. I just thought you might be hungry."

"Well, at least pour yourself some coffee."

Wes nodded and poured himself some from the pot. He started to go out.

"Sit with me for a minute, Wes."

He hesitated and then turned and slid into a chair.

Still moves like a panther.

"Tell me why you're really here. Are you broke? Need a place to crash? Hopin' to cash in when I'm gone?"

Wes looked at Josie sadly. Then he reached into his pocket and pulled out his checkbook. He opened it and showed her the balance—$60,000.

"I don't need your money, Josie. I don't need your stuff. I'm here to make amends for what I did to you in the past and to help you as best as I can to get through this terrible thing you're going through. I got my own food and everything I need in my trailer. I'll stay until it's over, and then I'll go my way. I'll take care of your stock, keep your place clean and make sure you got plenty of firewood for the winter. I'll be here if you need me and if not, I'll be out back. When the time comes, I'll be your caregiver."

Josie stared at Wes. "But why? I don't like you one bit. In fact, a long time ago, I decided I hated you as much as a woman could hate a man. You chewed me up and spit me out, Wes. Left me with a baby and an old silver locket. Took off with a cheap blonde and never looked back. Why, in God's name, should I believe anything you are saying?"

Wes looked down at his coffee. "Every word you say is true and I know you got good reason to hate my guts." He looked up. "I'm just hopin' that maybe someday you can find it in your heart to forgive me."

She almost laughed out loud. Then she zeroed in. "But why? Why are you here? Tell me so I can get a handle on this."

"I got my reasons, Josie. Someday I'll tell you, but not today. So here it is. You're alone, you got no one. Pretty soon you're going to be so sick you won't be able to get out of that bed. I'm sorry. It breaks my heart to see it happen to you, but there's nothing you or I can do about it. So, I'm here. What you see is what you get. I'll do the best I can to make it easier for you, and then I'll go. I don't want nothing from you in return." He got up. "Let me know what you decide. If it's no, I'll be on my way today." He stopped at the back door. "I'll be in the trailer."

<hr>

Josie sat at the kitchen table for a long time. She didn't have the faintest idea what she should do, but her curiosity was growing. She had no idea why Wes was here, his explanation aside. She kept thinking about how improbable, preposterous this whole deal was. She drank more coffee and tried to figure it all out.

Maybe if I let him stay for a week or so, he'll slip up and show me what he's up to.

Around noon she had another round with the "It," but the morphine made it at least bearable. She dressed and went out to feed Salty. She found him fed, brushed, watered, and his stall mucked out.

That would have taken me a while.

She heard an axe hitting wood and went out the barn door. Wes was by the woodpile with his sleeves rolled up past his biceps. He'd rolled a big round out and was splitting smaller rounds on it. He already had a good pile of split firewood going.

The axe moved with a curious rhythm, swish, thump, pause, swish, thump, pause. Wes looked fit, not an ounce of fat on him. His shoulders filled the Pendleton shirt, and the muscles rippled on his bare arms as he swung. Josie remembered those powerful arms carrying her. She shoved the feeling away.

Wes looked up and laid the axe aside. "Well, what do you want to do, Josie?"

She flushed and looked away.

What am I doing?

She looked back. "I've been thinking. What if you stayed for a week and we see how it works out? You're right about the place. I could have handled it before I got sick, but I have to sit a lot now."

He laughed. "Going to give me some time to let my angle slip?"

She blushed. "Why, I…"

"Come on, Josie. We were married. I know the way you think. But it's okay. I'm happy to stay until you see I ain't lying, or you throw me out. One or the other."

She looked down. "Okay, then." It was a whisper.

"I'll finish this and then I want to work on the gingerbread on the front porch. Some broken pieces. I looked around in the barn and found some spare sections I can cannibalize. Got any paint that matches?"

She nodded. "I think so."

"Right. We'll give it a week."

"A week. Okay."

She turned and walked back into the barn.

What in the world am I doing?

Chapter Six

TENDER MERCIES...

A week went by. Wes was still there. Early morning. Josie sat in the kitchen, staring at the wall, something she had been doing a lot. Her stomach twisted, but it wasn't pain. It was Wes. He had a way of doing that. When he was around, she felt her teeth on edge. She didn't want him close to her, but she didn't want him to leave.

It wasn't as though he had said anything or been untoward in his behavior toward her. He had been a perfect gentleman. And that's what bugged her. Wes Branson had never been a perfect gentleman in his life.

You are giving me the twitch, Wes Branson.

There was a knock on the kitchen door.

"Come in."

Wes poked his head around the door. "Did you see the weather report on TV? Looks like we're going to have an Indian summer, right through to the end of September."

"So?"

"I heard there's a river near here that has some nice trout. The Blitzer? Something like that."

"Actually, it's Donner und Blitzen. It means thunder and lightning."

Wes shook his head. "That's the one. I got some gear in my trailer. Thought you might like to take the day and go fly fishing."

"Wes Branson, I've never been fly fishing in my life."

Wes grinned. "Time you learned. Besides, you can't sit in the kitchen all day drinking coffee and staring at the wall."

Josie stared at him.

You got that right, Bud.

"Okay, I'll go. What do I need?"

"I think I've got everything. Extra rod, flies, nets, waders… course they might be a little big. But I won't get you out in water that's too deep. You'll need some jeans, bring an extra pair in case you fall in. Sweatshirt, jacket, socks, you know, like camping for a day. Oh, and bring a couple pair of thick socks to fill out the waders."

Suddenly Josie was excited. It sounded like a lot of fun.

"Okay. Give me a few minutes to throw some things together."

"Great, we'll take my truck."

AN HOUR LATER, they pulled off the Frenchglen Highway onto Krumbo Reservoir Road. In about ten minutes, they pulled up beside a lovely stream. Wes got the rods out of the back. They were already set up. He handed her a pair of hip waders.

"They are just big galoshes. Put on those extra thick socks you brought and then we'll get them on and fasten them to your belt."

Wes got her fixed up with the waders and then he spent a half hour showing her how to cast. They waded out into the stream. Josie was a natural. She loved being away from the house, just being out here, away from the "It." The sun was bright, but not too hot. The river was smooth, green, cracked ice when the sun hit it.

Wes left her in a flat spot and moved downstream. She was casting for a few minutes when she felt a tug on her fly. She yelled. He turned. She had a trout on. She lifted the tip of the rod to show him and the fish came out of the water.

Wes lifted his hand to stop her, but the fish used the tension on the line and flipped right off into the river. He laughed at the look on her face. He waded over and tapped her net.

"In here first, Josie. Then show me." He grinned.

She watched as he moved downstream and cast his fly in along the riverbank, under some low hanging bushes. BOOM! The fish came right out of the water and his pole bent under the weight of a big trout. He reeled in expertly, grabbed his net with his left hand and dipped it under. He lifted the wriggling fish to show her.

Josie felt the old competitive spirit rise in her.

He's not gonna get more fish than me.

She waded out toward the middle of the river, headed for the bank on the opposite side. She stepped out where the current was stronger and then the bottom dropped out from under her. She went in over her head and her waders filled, pulling her down. She hit the bottom and shoved up with all her might. Her head broke the surface, and she screamed.

"WES!"

Down she went again, but this time the water in her boots held her down. She looked up at the sun shining through the surface, broken, like flames of fire.

Maybe this is better…

And then powerful hands grasped her outstretched arms, and she broke the surface.

Wes!

"I got you, Josie, I got you. I won't let go."

His powerful arms wrapped around her and he was dragging her through the river. She felt him lift her and carry her up on the bank and her arms went around him and she held him with all her strength.

"Wes! Wes."

"I got you, honey. I got you. I won't let go."

He held her to his brawny chest. She could feel his heart pounding.

"Josie, Josie."

They stayed that way for a long time.

She changed into her dry clothes while Wes changed his. They did it with their backs to each other, silent, quick. Josie didn't think she liked what she felt when Wes held her.

How did I get into this?

The drive home was silent, Josie looking out the window, Wes staring straight ahead. Finally, Josie spoke. "I think you should go, Wes. I think you should pack up and go."

He glanced over at her, then went back to staring. "Whatever you say, Josie."

There was silence for another five miles. Then Josie spoke.

"Why did you leave me, Wes?"

There! It's out on the table.

Wes looked out the window and when he looked back, there were two tears running down his cheeks.

I never, ever, saw you cry.

"Can we pull over and talk, Josie?"

"Whatever."

He pulled the truck into a turnout and switched off the engine. They sat for a long time. Finally, Wes turned to Josie.

"I left because I didn't know."

"Didn't know what?"

"I didn't know anything. How to be a husband, a father, be

responsible, keep a bank account, make something of my life. I never learned."

"Didn't your dad tell you anything?"

"My dad was a wildcatter. He followed the oil. Texas, Colorado, California, Venezuela, Alaska… anywhere there was oil my dad went after it. He was never home. I never knew him."

"What about your mom?"

"A mom can't teach a young boy how to be a man. She tried, but she didn't know what I needed to hear. She couldn't come to the Junior Rodeo and brag me up to the other dads when I won. She… she was good, but I needed more." He sighed. "Oh, he'd come home. Once a year, Thanksgiving, Christmas. And when he did, he would get drunk and whup me. He was never faithful to my mother. He had a girl-friend in every town. What he taught me was that a real man doesn't love women, he conquers them. When I was sixteen, an oil derrick collapse in Saudi Arabia killed him."

"So, what does that have to do with me?"

"When he died, everything he was, and everything he wasn't… that was my inheritance. That's all he left me. I didn't know how to be good to you. I didn't know how to take care of you. You were only seventeen. You didn't need to be with me. You were too young."

Josie thought about that. He was wrong.

"I had to be with you."

Wes looked surprised. "What do you mean?"

"Besides the fact that I was madly in love with you… I guess you can call it that… I needed you to take me away from where I was."

"I know, because of Ted?"

Josie looked out the window. The memory…

SHE HATED this time of night. When it was dark, when her mother was sleeping. She would lie in her bed in the dark, nowhere to go, staring at the ceiling, mouth dry. The waiting was the worst. Knowing that he was coming, knowing what would happen, anticipating the smell of his breath, listening to his lies...

"YOU KNOW I just had to get out, Wes. That's all. I don't want to talk about it. Maybe you're right. Maybe I was too young, but I needed someone to save me."

"It was terrible what happened to you. And the guy claiming to be a Christian."

Josie almost laughed. "Right, a Christian. Looked good at church, always the glad-hander, a deacon. What a joke. He was a total hypocrite. If he was a Christian, I don't want any of it."

"I knew talking about Christians put you off your feed. I should have put two and two together. But back then, I was barely conscious most of the time..."

Josie twisted in her seat. "I said I didn't want to talk about it!" She almost screamed.

He stopped talking.

She took a deep breath. "Besides, we were talking about you. Why you left. I had a baby, I had nothing. You didn't even look back. You headed off on the rodeo tour with some blonde. Damn, Wes. How could you do that to me?"

Wes looked over at her, and his face was a study in remorse. "I was messed up, Josie. I'm sorry. You'll never know how sorry I am." He stopped, took a breath. "The sad part is I didn't even have a reason to leave, at least not one I could articulate. I just did it. Of course, I know now I was too young. I couldn't handle the responsibility. But that doesn't excuse it. I was wrong, totally, incredibly wrong. I hurt you deeply, and it's been one of the hardest things in my life to deal with. I hope... I said it before. I hope that someday you can forgive me."

Josie shook her head and looked back out the window.

"Wes Branson, it will be a cold day in hell before I forgive you."

There. I said it.

"Now, would you just take me home?"

When they pulled up at the house, Wes stopped and let her out. "I'll be gone in the morning."

Josie leaned back in and looked at him. "You should have let me drown, Wes." She closed the truck door and walked into the house.

———

THAT NIGHT, she had the memory again. The dark room, the quiet steps in the hallway. The door opened and a little light from the front room came in. She could see him in the half-light. She wanted to hide, but there was nowhere to go. He came and stood by the bed. He took hold of the covers and turned them back. Then it was different... different because...

... the door burst open and someone else came in. Someone who had never been in the memory. There was the sound of a fist hitting bone, another. A grunt, like a gut-shot deer. She heard a thud and then a heavy body being dragged out of the room. Shouting. Her mother screaming. A door slamming, a car roaring down the driveway. She heard steps. She cowered under the covers, then looked out. Someone was standing in the doorway, the light all around him. No darkness, no fear, only... Wes.

She woke up sweating. The "It" was racking her body. She stumbled from her bed and staggered to the bathroom. She threw up, hard, retching, sobs tearing her gut.

He saved me. Wes saved me.

Wait... no, he didn't save me; he killed me. It was just a dream.

She fumbled a pain pill out of the jar and washed it down with water from the tap.

She remembered him holding her at the river... for a long time, his arms strong but gentle, his face next to hers. He had whispered her name and there was so much tenderness.

Josie! Josie.

There was love there in his voice. She could hear it. She could feel it in the way he held her.

NO!

She staggered out of the bathroom into the front room.

"I don't want him to love me. I don't want to love him! I want to hate him!"

Josie Winters sank down on the couch and sobbed and sobbed...

Chapter Seven

HARD ROADS

*J*osie awakened early. She could hear Wes doing something out by the barn. She got up, slipped on her bathrobe, and peeked through the venetian blinds. He was down on one knee, hitching his trailer up.

He's leaving. He's really leaving.

Suddenly Josie was in a panic. She stripped off her robe and pajamas, slipped into some jeans and a sweatshirt and ran a brush through her hair.

Wait, Josie. You want him to leave.

She paused in the middle of a stroke. And then it was clear as a bell.

Wes Branson is the only person in this world who cares about me. I could feel it at the river when he saved me. I... I need him to stay.

She finished brushing her hair and went out through the kitchen door. Wes looked up as she approached and then went back to his hitch.

She stopped a few feet away and watched him. No wasted motions, everything smooth, much different from the nineteen-year-old kid she had married.

He finished and stood up. "Mornin', Josie."

"Wes."

He looked at her. She expected recrimination on his face, but there was only kindness in his eyes.

"Sorry about your fishing rod. I think it went down the river."

He shrugged. "I can get another."

"Where are you going?"

"Back to Texas. There's a job waiting for me."

"With the rodeo?"

"No, wrangling for an outfit outside of Amarillo. Pay's good, I ride every day." He smiled and started toward the truck.

"You leaving right now?"

"In a few minutes. Got to check the trailer connections."

"Wes..." She took hold of his arm. He stopped and looked away, then back.

"What is it, Josie?"

"I don't... I can't..."

He turned and put his hands on her shoulders. Powerful hands. She could feel their warmth.

"What do you want to say, Josie?"

"I'm confused, Wes. I want to hate you. I want to hurt you, like you hurt me. But..."

He smiled a part-way smile. "You are hurting me, Josie. More than you know."

"How? How am I hurting you?"

"You're dying. Dammit, Josie. You're dying. And that hurts."

She stared at him. This was not the callous boy that had walked out without ever looking back. This was a man. A real man. She could see his life on his face, in his eyes. She could see the caring, and suddenly she needed that more than she needed to live.

"Wes... please."

She just looked and then suddenly she was in his arms, weeping, sobbing. "Wes, Wes, please don't go. I need you. I need you... please.."

His arms tightened around her and he was stroking her hair. "It's okay, Josie. Don't cry, honey. I'll stay. I'll stay."

***

SHE SAT for a long time in the kitchen that afternoon. She could hear him outside, whistling. Every note of the song was perfect.

I don't think he even knows that he whistles Tumblin' Tumbleweeds when he works.

She smiled without thinking.

I know him well, but... I don't know him. Something's changed in him.

She felt empty. She didn't know why. This whole thing with Wes. She realized that despite the years of anger that she didn't hate him anymore.

Maybe the hate being gone left this empty place?

She guessed that just the few simple things he had done for her, saving her life aside, had touched something in her. The place he touched was raw, but she couldn't turn away from the touch. Josie Winters had hardened herself over the years. She didn't like people, especially church people, she didn't like rodeo men, she didn't like...

I don't like anything and that killed me a long time ago. Now I'm just catching up to my funeral.

There was a knock on the kitchen door.

"Come."

She heard the screen squeak. Then the door opened. Wes came in with a big cast-iron frying pan and a few assorted paper bags.

"What are you up to now?"

She didn't like the snarky tone of her voice, so she tried again.

"Sorry, Wes. What's up?"

He smiled that half-smile. It made him look younger than he was.

"When you fell in the river, I pitched my pole up on the bank. When I went back for it, the trout was still on."

He reached into one bag and pulled out a big, very big trout.

"Sixteen inches, about four pounds. Should make some good eating. Want to try?"

"I've never been much of a fish person…"

"Josie, there are fish and then there are trout. I guarantee you will be riding a different horse when this parade is finished."

She grinned and nodded. "Okay, go ahead. What can I do?"

"You got salad makin's?"

Josie got up and went to the frig, looked in. "Yeah, I got some lettuce that still looks good, a couple of tomatoes, some green peppers… oh there's a cuke and I only bought it three days ago."

"We're good then."

"Shouldn't we have some wine or something with it?"

Wes shrugged. "When I stopped lookin' on the booze, the sun came up after a long night. So, I don't put myself back in the way of that train anymore, whether it's hard or soft. But if you got some, you're welcome, won't bother me. I made some sweet tea."

I never knew you not to take a drink. What's going on here?

"You got some bacon in there. Want to get it out?"

Josie rummaged in the meat drawer and pulled out a package of bacon. "Okay."

"Pull me off four strips. And I'll take that last lime you got in there. You know, the Corona lime."

Josie blushed but handed it over.

"Perfect. Now you get busy on the salad while I dress this troutski up for the ball."

She watched as he gutted the trout and then used his filet knife to cut two nice filets from the sides of the big trout.

"Turn the oven on to four hundred, would you?"

She did as he requested, and then got busy with the salad, but she still watched him. He seasoned the filets with salt and pepper and then put two slices of bacon over it.

"Oh, I forgot. Got any cooking oil?"

She went to the cupboard and got out a jar of olive oil.

"Perfect."

He put the cast-iron pan on the stove and heated the oil. When it was hot, he added the trout, cooked it until the bacon was nicely browned. He turned the filets over and put the whole pan in the oven.

"Better get going on that salad. The fish will be done in about ten minutes."

Josie bent herself to her task. It felt good doing this with Wes. Natural. Easy. She remembered how he used to be so competitive. Everything had to be his way. But not now. This was like that Eagles song, a peaceful, easy feeling...

The timer on the oven dinged, and he took out the fish. It smelled wonderful.

"Give me that lime, Jose."

She handed him the lime. He had always called her Jose. It was his pet name. It felt good.

"Plates?"

She rustled some out of the cupboard and got out some silverware and glasses. There were some jars of salad dressing in the frig and she got those out—Thousand Island, Ranch, Italian.

He deftly cut the lime in half and squeezed each half onto a piece of fish. She set the table and they sat down. He pulled out a jar with tea in it and poured himself a glass.

Josie held out her glass. "I'll have some of that, too."

He poured her some and then set the jar down. "Do you mind if I say grace?"

She looked at him. "Didn't know you were a grace kinda guy."

He shrugged. "I lived with some praying people for a time and kind of got in the habit. If you mind, I won't."

"No, go ahead."

He kept it simple. "Bless this to our use. Amen."

They dug in.

Josie had never tasted anything quite like this trout. It was scrumptious. She piled some salad on her plate and poured on some Italian.

He's going to put Thousand Island on his...

He did.

They ate quietly, and then they were done. She looked at him across the table.

"Thank you, Wes. That was absolutely delicious."

He reddened and looked down. "Glad you liked it, Jose."

"I have some ice cream, if you'd like a little desert."

He nodded. "You know me. Ice cream and horses make the world go round."

She paused.

I know you. But I don't know you, either.

They had their ice cream with only a few words between them. She watched him. He had grown into a lovely man. Tall, extremely handsome, he had been gangly when he was a kid, but now all the gangle was gone, replaced by muscles that filled his shirt.

His face had changed the most. When Wes left her, his face had been soft, almost feminine, with none of the character she saw there now. Now it was a grown man's face, angles and lines, some of them from laughing, some that looked deeper, more personal. She had decided after a couple of days that she liked the mustache, but she wondered about the scar it hid. It was a nasty scar, almost big enough to mar his face, but not quite.

"How'd you get the scar?"

He shifted in his chair. "After I left Laredo, I tried the rodeo for a couple of years, but I was never quite fast enough or tough enough to take home the silver belt. So, I hit the road."

Josie felt a little bitter taste come up in her throat. "What about the blonde?"

He looked away. "Not something I'm proud of. I never made enough money to suit her, so she was gone in about six weeks."

Josie looked down. She had embarrassed him and she felt bad. "Sorry. Let's go back to the scar."

"Well, I joined the Marines."

He smiled at the shocked expression on her face.

"The war was on and it was 1967. You had to either join up or get drafted. So, I joined up. I ended up in the 5th Marine Regiment, 1st Battalion, 1st Marines. They shipped us off to Nam almost as soon as we finished our training. On January 31, 1968, the communists took control of Hue, a major South Vietnamese city. They sent us over to dig them out. We got there on February 14. I was in Delta Company and the brass sent us to spearhead the attack. We moved into the Citadel, a fortified section of the old city, and began our assault at daybreak on February 15. We were used to fighting in dense jungle, so combat in those tightly packed streets was disorienting to most of us. Sounds ricocheted off walls and confused us. Crumbled buildings and blind corners made perfect sniper nests and ambush points. It was chaos."

Wes took a sip of his tea. Josie could see this was very hard.

"After some tough fighting, Delta Company regrouped at Dang Ba Tower. The strategy was simple. We needed the tower as an observation point, so they told us to charge the tower, kill all the enemy, and hold it. It seemed simple. But the place was alive with North Vietnamese Army regulars. They were in sniper foxholes and behind rubble. When we were going in, they let us have it. My buddy, Steve Connors, went down with bullets in his legs. Luis, my other buddy, got shot up real bad. I picked him up and dragged him out to an aid station. I was going back for Steve when a mass of rocket and mortar fire lit us up. Shrapnel hit me in the face and knocked me out. When I woke up, I dragged myself back to the tower. Steve was dead. More rounds came in and knocked the building down around us. I woke up in a field hospital with my legs full of metal and a mortar kiss on my face. That bowlegged you see when I'm walking didn't all come from bustin' broncs."

Wes took a deep breath. "That's the story. Anything else you'd like to know?" But it wasn't a defensive question, it was genuine.

Josie put her face in her hands. Then looked up. "We missed a lot of each other, didn't we?"

Wes nodded.

"Does Margarita know about your service days?"

Wes smiled. "Margarita and I are doing well. I've shared a lot."

"Why didn't you ever contact me?"

"Josie, I knew you hated me. I wanted to. I can't tell you how many times I picked up a phone to get in touch, but... okay, can I be honest?"

She looked at him and nodded.

"I was afraid. Me, Wes Branson, Mr. Tough Guy, wounded vet, rodeo rider... I was afraid. What happened between us was my fault, and my fault alone. And it took me a long time to face up to it. I figured you were doing okay, so I just let it ride. And then I heard you were sick, and I had to come. So here I am."

Josie stood up. "You know, Wes, I thought I had toughened up over the years, but all this... well, it's hard. I need to think about it. But... we'll talk some more if that's okay."

He smiled, and the relief was palpable. "Sure, Jose. Any time. I got all the time..."

He stopped. "I mean... oh shoot, Jose, I'm not good at this. But yeah, we'll talk. Let me help with the dishes."

She smiled. "I got it. I need to be alone. You go ahead on."

"Okay, goodnight."

Wes got up and went out the door.

Wesley James Branson, war hero. Who'd of guessed?

Chapter Eight

HUMMINGBIRDS

osie woke up. It was dark in her room, very dark—that hour before the gray that precedes dawn pushes the stars out of the sky and slips through the window. She lay there wondering what had awakened her. And then she heard it. It was music, a song, a low, rich voice singing, a guitar plucking soft chords. Wes!

The words were faint and indistinct. She slipped out of bed and went to the closet, pulled down her robe. Josie wrapped it around her, a shield against the chill of the November dawn. She slid her feet into some loafers and went out into the dark of the front room. Making her way softly through the kitchen, she quietly opened the back door and went out.

Wes's voice grew louder as she walked to the trailer. She could hear the words now. It was real country, like a Willie Nelson song, but she had never heard it before. She listened. The words came, dropping into her heart one by one, like small bits of water in an April rain.

They were good days
Sweet times
Hot summer nights and

Dream times
Layin' in the grass
With my head in the stars
There was promise in your kiss
And forever in your arms

HE STOPPED and then started again. At the beginning.

He's writing a song.

She went to the door of the trailer, lifted her hand to knock, and then suddenly she was weak and sick. She lowered her hand.

It's private. I'm not part of that anymore.

She turned and went back to the house. Inside, she went to the bathroom and took a pill. Then she took off her robe and crawled back into her bed. She lay there for a long time, staring into the dark. And she remembered the music days...

WES BRANSON WAS one of those naturals, a musician who didn't know how good he was, who never thought of himself that way. In his mind he was just another singing cowboy, with the emphasis on cowboy.

After they were together, Wes encouraged her to sing. He had at least given her that. She had a rich contralto voice that blended perfectly with his, but when he showed her how to get there, she discovered she could sing second soprano too. She remembered Wes laughing the first time she expanded her range from one and a half octaves to three. There was something about singing that took away all the dark places of her past, the night memories and the shakes.

Wes never took lessons. He just picked up a guitar one day when he was a kid and jumped in. He started out as a kid tenor, but by the time he was nineteen, his voice was moving towards a

Jim Reeves bass. Wes wrote songs. She remembered the little notebook he kept where he jotted down ideas.

Hummingbirds. The first song we ever wrote together.

The hummingbirds danced the day they met. She was a town girl, he was a rodeo cowboy. They met at the Laredo / Webb County 4th of July Fair in the summer of 1962. Josie was at the animal barn, wandering from stall to stall, looking at the horses and dreaming. She didn't want to be around her mom and step-dad. She wanted to enjoy the fair without the vapid, gossipy comments from her mother and the unwanted touches from Ted, so she rode the bus so she would have the day to herself. Now she was looking at the horses and wondering what it would be like to own one.

"You like horses?"

The voice at her shoulder made her jump. She held onto the bar of the stall and slowly turned. A handsome, dark-haired young man in a black cowboy hat and a western shirt was standing there with a smile on his face. What caught her were the eyes, blue... like the Rio Grande as it flowed slowly through Big Bend Park.

"Didn't mean to scare you."

"You didn't." She turned away.

"So, was that little jump just something you do in an exercising sort of way?"

She turned back. He still had laughter in his eyes. "Okay, you startled me. Why are you sneaking up on a girl like that, anyway? You a perv or something?"

"Well, maybe." He grinned again. It was rather infuriating. "Actually, I just wanted to know if you like horses."

"Dumb question. What would I be doing down here in this smelly barn if I didn't?"

"Do you ride?"

"Is that any of your business?"

"Didn't mean no offense. I just thought you might like to see some real horses."

He piqued her interest. "Real horses?"

"Yeah. Buckin' broncs. Mean. Nasty, chain lightin' on the hoof. Big, strong, right off the range. Not like these little pets down here."

"Why are you here then?"

He nodded toward the door. "Just taking a shortcut to the rodeo barn. Want to come?"

Josie hesitated and then nodded her head.

"Well, come on then."

And that was the beginning.

His name was Wesley James Branson. He was trying to get on to the rodeo circuit. In the meantime, he was working at a feed store to get by. He was on his own and getting established. He chatted about the rodeo as they walked, how he had been to a school where the bronc-riding veterans had given the rookies tips.

"Yeah, we learned some good stuff. Did you know that even if you ride a horse every day, that still doesn't get you in shape to ride a bucking horse? You need to whip yourself into shape so when you're fighting the jolts, or you get tossed off on your head, your body is in condition to take it. You should lift weights and stretch a lot, do cardio exercise. It's a lot of work. I'm trying to do it as much as I can."

She snuck a peek at his slim, muscular body and decided he was definitely keeping up with his program. They came to the bronc barn and he walked her through. A couple of older looking cowboys nodded to Wes as they walked.

"The big guy, that's Randy Garrison. He's been to the National Finals rodeo three times. That's what I'm hoping to do."

He showed her the different bucking horses. "This one is

called Lazy Susan, because she sneaks up on you. When she busts out of the gate, she'll spend a few seconds making you think she's on a Sunday ride. Then she explodes and starts whirling around like one of those things on a kitchen table. If you can stay on for even three more seconds, you're better than most."

Josie liked Wes. He was attentive; he was good-looking. He was full of himself, but she didn't mind. Wes seemed nice and she liked that.

After they toured the barn, he asked her if she wanted to go get something to eat. It was a beautiful south Texas night. The fairgrounds were full of people—cowboys and cowgirls, families, Mexican folks from across the river in Nuevo Laredo. The air was filled with noise and music. A mariachi band was blasting away down by the Ferris wheel and a country band was playing "Crazy" on the arena stage. The sounds intertwined in the air.

It was moving toward dusk and the sky slowly filled with beautiful pink clouds, touched by the purple and rose of the coming sunset and the last rays of the sun as it slipped into the crack where tomorrow lives.

Josie sighed. "It's beautiful tonight. The sky is like the honeysuckle flowers in my back yard. All pink and purple. A honeysuckle sky."

Wes looked at her. "That's nice." He took out a little notepad from his shirt pocket and a stub of pencil. He wrote and then stuck it back in the pocket.

"What's that?"

He reddened. "I play a little guitar and I like to write songs. I jot down good lyric ideas. That was one. Honeysuckle sky. Good one."

They walked down the midway to the food vendors. They each got a corn dog with lots of mustard and a coke. Wes grinned. "I'd like something a little stronger, but they won't sell it to me here."

They walked around, looking for a place to sit. They found a bench by a wall covered with bougainvillea vines. The flaming red flowers were alive with hummingbirds. They sat and watched. The birds darted here and there seeking the nectar, their wings whirring. Two of them flew straight up into the sky, twisting and turning in perfect synchronized flight against the beautiful sky.

Josie watched. "They're dancing. The hummingbirds are dancing in the honeysuckle sky."

She looked at Wes. He was staring at her. He reached over and took her hand. A shock went through her. His touch was gentle, but he had claimed her fingers and she didn't want him to let go.

"Josie, can I give you a ride home?"

She didn't want to go home, not yet. Not with her stepdad there. "Yes, but not yet. I don't want to go home yet."

"Want to see the fireworks, then?"

"Yes. Please."

They wandered hand in hand to a small hill by the fairgrounds fence. It had grown dark. The sky filled with stars, bright points of light that the glare of the midway hardly dimmed. They sat together for a long time. She shivered, even though it was still very warm. Wes put his arm around her and for the first time in almost her whole life, she felt safe.

They sat that way for a long time. Then, from the fairgrounds, they heard the announcer's voice prepping the fireworks show. In a moment, it began. Bright explosions rocked the sky. Purples, reds, giant fireballs, blazing torches—the sky filled with wonder. Then there was a pause and a single rocket went up. Up, up, way up, and then the explosion and the night sky filled with a thousand falling silver stars.

"The stars are falling, Wes, the stars are falling down."

Wes turned and bent to her. Their lips met and her heart gave a huge leap. Her arms went around him and she held him as tightly as she could. "Wes, Wes, don't let me go, don't ever let me go."

"I won't, Josie, I won't."

But he did.

JOSIE WOKE. She was damp with sweat, but night sweats had become part of "It". She lay for a long time staring at the ceiling. She had loved Wes, or so she thought. When he left, her world had collapsed.

Was it really love? Or did I just want to get away from home? From Ted?

She rolled over.

WES TOOK her home late that first night. After the fireworks, they walked around the midway, hand in hand. He won a small bear for her at a baseball toss booth. They had another corn dog, some lemonade, they did a bunch of nothing things, but her day was full of treasure. He held her hand and every little while, he stopped and kissed her. She loved his kisses. They were real; they came from somewhere new and lovely... Finally, she told him she had to go. He had an old white pickup with some rusted out spots, but it ran smooth and quiet. They drove slowly through the night. She sat as close to him as she could get.

Her stepfather was already in bed and her mom was sitting at the kitchen table, three empty martini glasses in front of her.

"Where have you been?" Not a question, really, because her mother didn't care where she'd been.

"I met someone. I'm going to marry him."

Her mother looked up, trying hard to focus.

Josie walked to the table.

"And I want you to tell Ted something."

"What, Josie?"

"Tell Ted if he ever comes in my room again at night, I will tell Wes, and Wes will kill him."

Her mother paled. "What do you mean?"

Josie put her face right in front of her mother's. "You know exactly what I mean," she whispered. Then she screamed. "YOU JUST TELL THAT…"

Josie's mom jerked to her feet. Her hand stopped the words with a hard slap. She stood trembling in front of Josie. "How dare you imply such a thing? Why Ted is decent, a Christian man. He would never…"

Josie scrabbled around in her purse and pulled out a condom. "Then why does he give me these?"

Josie's mother looked at her and then at the thing in her hand.

Josie watched her mother's eyes and she understood at last.

She got right into her mother's face. Her mother tried to look away…

"You knew."

It was more like a question. Then…

"You knew, didn't you? You knew he was doing that to me. And you let him."

Josie's mother sank into the chair. She put her hands over her face. She sat that way, hiding.

"Mom?"

Her mother's voice was barely audible. "He said he would leave me if I said anything."

"What?"

"He said he would leave me."

Josie grabbed her mother's hands and pulled, jerked them out of the way. "Look at me!"

Her mother looked up. Tears ran down her face. "Josie… Josie… I…"

"How could you? How…? He was… he was doing that to your own daughter and you knew. YOU KNEW!"

Ragged breath… pounding heart…

"And all the time you were parading around that stinking church like you were some kind of holy…"

She choked on the thought.

Josie stood for a long time, shaking, staring at her mother.

Then getting her breath. Steadying. At last, she took her mother's face gently in her hands and whispered in her ear.

"You just tell him what I said about Wes."

She and Wes were married a month later.

Chapter Nine

HIDDEN PLACES

The sun was pale, barely breaking through a winter haze. Josie woke in a cold room. She could hear Wes out in the living room. There was a thump... another.

He's building a fire.

She had a morphine hangover. In the night, she had taken an extra pill to knock herself out, but it had taken a long time to put her to sleep. She looked at the alarm clock beside her bed.

Ten o'clock. I better get up.

The pain in her side was a dull ache this morning, occasionally punctuated with electric twinges and sharp needles of fire. She swung her feet over the side of the bed and sat until the cold drove her to get up. Slow shuffle across to the closet, robe, slippers. Got a pill from the bathroom stash, ran her fingers through her hair. Looked in the mirror.

I look like hammered...

Another thump from the front room.

Must have dropped a log.

Josie turned on the cold water and splashed it on her face. She toweled off and grabbed her brush. As she brushed, she noticed a clump of hair in the bristles.

Great. Now my hair's coming out.

Suddenly, the weight of everything crushed down. She stumbled to the bed, sat, put her face in her hands and sobbed.

In a few seconds, there was a knock on the door.

"Josie? You okay?"

She roused herself, went to the door, and opened it. Wes was there with a troubled look on his face. "You okay? Did you hurt yourself?"

She looked at him for a long time, then it came out.

"Oh, Wes! I don't want to die."

He stepped forward and pulled her close. She sank into him, clinging like a drowning woman, the sobs wracked her.

"There now, girl. I know. I don't want you to die, either. I'd give anything..." He stopped.

The sobs quieted. She snuffled against his shoulder.

"Why, Wes? Why do you care? Easing your conscience? Paying an old debt? Why would you care about a worn-out old hag like me? You didn't back then. You just waltzed off like you were going out for some smokes. But you never came back, you never came back. And now you're here and I don't have the faintest idea why."

"I'm here because..." He stopped and swallowed hard. "Come on. I got a nice fire going, coffee on the stove. You can sit and warm yourself and we'll talk."

The blaze in the fireplace was comforting. There was a stack of wood piled to the side, and the warmth was already taking the chill off. Wes led her to the couch and fetched a thick woolen blanket off a chest in the corner. She put her legs up under her and he tucked her in. She loved the pampered feeling.

"Back in a minute."

He went into the kitchen and she heard him bustling around, the clink of cups, the little gurgle of coffee out of the pot. Then he was back with a tray—two mugs, a little pitcher of cream and some sugar. He set it on the end table by her and took one of the mugs, the blue one. He left her the red one.

He remembered

Wes started to go sit in one of the big comfy chairs, but she reached out and took his sleeve.

"Sit by me, Wes. I'm lonely this morning."

So he sat. She motioned him to sit closer, and he did. They sat for a while, just enjoying the fire, the coffee, and the unsullied quiet. Finally, he put his coffee down and clasped his hands together in front of him, leaned on his knees.

"Why am I here? That's a big question. But I think first I need to tell you where I went, where I've been. Okay?"

She nodded. She had wanted to hear this for so long, and then for a long time she didn't care. So many feelings for one man —burning love, cold steel hate, indifference, forgetfulness, the empty ache, the desperate attempts to fill the hole in her heart. Oh yeah, he had taken a sizable piece of her when he left. And now here he was.

Do I really want to hear this?

You need to.

Josie looked around at Wes. "Did you say something?"

He smiled, the half smile, like whatever joy there might be in his life did not quite fill the bucket. "Not yet."

"Oh, I thought you did." She looked away. "I was just thinking I wanted to hear this for so long and then I didn't care. So, go easy, cause I'm tender."

He nodded. "I'll go as easy as I can. Okay. Where did I go? Where have I been..."

***

WES BRANSON PUT the last of his clothing into the battered suitcase. He looked around at the apartment. It was on the ratty side of Laredo and not really a place to raise a kid, but it was all he could afford. Margi was at the sitter's house and Josie was out working at the House of Whiskey down by the river. She'd been there for three months now, but the finances had not improved that much. Wes looked around.

Nothin' to keep me.

He picked up the suitcase and his guitar and went out of the house to his truck. A brazen blonde was sitting in the passenger seat.

"What took you so long, Wessy?"

He didn't like her calling him that, but he said nothing. Wes had the feeling he was in over his head and didn't quite know how he'd gotten here.

He met Veda at the feed store where he worked. She was the front desk girl, and she had a way of filling her blouse that caught Wes's eye. Veda was a rodeo groupie, and she made over Wes's ambitions to ride in the National. One thing led to another and the next thing he knew, he was in up to his neck in a clandestine affair. He didn't call it a love affair, because he didn't love Veda. The physical part was all right, and she puffed his ego.

He was pretty sure he loved Josie, but she had been a real pain lately. She was always complaining about the money, or lack thereof, and she made a big stink when Wes told her she had to go to work. And she was on his case all the time about his drinking.

Within two months after they were married, Wes was on his way to being an alcoholic. He always had at least a six-pack in the frig, and he loved to do straight tequila shots with Corona chasers. When their baby was born, he was drunk. He named her Margarita. He wrote it on the birth certificate before Josie could object.

She had complained about that. She had complained about his working late, even though she didn't realize that there was more to it than just putting in some overtime. The day he came home with his paycheck and told her he didn't make enough and she was going to have to go to work, she freaked out. Of course, he had stopped at the bar first to take on a little liquid courage.

Josie was not happy at his announcement. "I want to stay home with Margi! I don't want to work. You're the man. You should make the money."

"Josie, I can't make enough at the feed store and I need extra to enter the events on the circuit."

"And that's another thing. You're gone every weekend. Fort Stockton, San Antonio, Belton. You come back all banged up, with a third-place ribbon, or sometimes nothing. A few bucks in prize money. Maybe it's time you faced up to your responsibilities. Quit this rodeo business. You've got a wife and a baby. And now you want me to go to work to make up the difference." Her voice went up in volume. "Well, I'm not going to…"

It was the first time he had slapped her. The look on her face twisted his guts, but he didn't back off.

"Now you listen to me. I don't make enough money yet so you need to help. You're going to get a job or so help me…"

"What? You'll beat me to death?"

There were tears in her eyes, but her face was hard like flint.

Wes ground his teeth and then spun on his heel and headed for the door.

"Now where are you going?"

"Out." The door slammed behind him.

It took a week for her to talk to him and by then she had gotten a job at a bar as a cocktail waitress. In the meantime, Veda had been putting the pressure on him.

"She don't want you to be a rodeo star, Wessy. Josie's so self-centered. She just wants you to get some dumb job in a factory or sellin' cars. Or stay home and take care of the kid. You was meant to be a big man. I can just see your name up on the big board at the Nationals. Wessy Branson, first place, bronc riding."

"It wouldn't say 'Wessy', Veda."

"I know, honey." She giggled. "I just think you could do a lot better. You and me could go places, do things. You'd be rich and famous, and I'd be your wife."

"Aren't you forgetting that I'm married?"

"Oh, that's easy, Wessy. Just divorce her."

"Then there would be alimony and child support. I can't even pay the bills now."

"Well, we could just take off. I know, let's go to California. They got rodeo there, too. We'll just disappear. By the time you get famous, she will have forgotten all about you. Oh, come on, Wessy, live a little." She snuggled up. "Don't you want me, honey?"

He guessed he did.

So now he was on his way out the door with a suitcase and a guitar and a blonde he didn't love eggin' him on. Of course, she left him six weeks after they got to California and he ran out of money.

"Oh, Wessy, it was fun, but Jimmy is already on the rodeo. I like you a lot, but a girl's got to look out for herself."

Josie looked over at Wes. "So that's how it happened? Some blonde with a big chest just dragged you off by the nose?"

Wes stared down at the floor. "I was mixed up, Josie. I thought I wanted to be a rodeo star, but I felt like you and the baby were holding me back."

"When she dumped you, why didn't you come back? I might have forgiven you."

Wes shook his head. "My pride and red likker got the best of me. I stayed drunk for a long time."

"But how did you live?"

"I got a job on a construction site. Lived in a motel in South LA. Got a few gigs playin' in country bars."

Wes got up and went to the kitchen. When he came back, he

had the coffeepot. "Warm up, hon?" He grinned. So did Josie. He poured some in their mugs.

Josie took a sip. "Then what happened, Wes?"

"Vietnam happened. And that's a whole 'nother conversation."

Josie looked over at Wes. He was still so handsome. The little scar just made him look... well, lived-in. "I love this, Wes. Well, not so much hearing about your affair, but just being here, talking. It wasn't as hard as I thought." Josie pondered for a moment. "Can we do this every morning for a while? It's winter and there won't be a lot to do outside."

Wes nodded. "Okay. I'm up for it... on one condition."

Josie looked over. "What?"

"You have to tell me your story, too."

She sat for a while thinking on that. "Are you sure? It's not a pretty picture."

Wes sighed. "I missed so much. I feel like a whole big chunk of my life disappeared into a black hole. It would help me." He smiled. "Maybe I didn't come here just to help you. Maybe we can help each other."

She nodded. "Okay... I'll try."

"Me too, Jose. Me too."

Chapter Ten

HUMMINGBIRDS FLY SOUTH

"Do you remember when we wrote Hummingbirds?"

They were sitting on the couch again. Winter had come on with a rush, and there was a six-inch dump of snow all around the house. Wes came in early that morning, got the fire going and fixed some pancakes. He got Josie fed and then went out and got Salty fed, too. Now they were sitting together, each with a mug of coffee, when Josie asked the question. They had promised to talk, but she wasn't quite ready to spill her guts, not yet. So she ambushed him.

Wes looked over. Surprisingly, there was genuine pain in his eyes. He swallowed hard and turned away for a minute. When he turned back, he was wiping a tear.

Josie just looked.

He is so tender. What happened to us? We missed so much.

Tell him what you see.

Josie didn't like the little promptings she had been getting. She didn't want to open any worm cans, but she bit the bullet and went ahead.

"You're crying."

He nodded. "It all just broke over me. I'm so sorry, Josie. So sorry for all we missed. When you asked about Hummingbirds, I went straight back to the night we met. You came up with those two wonderful word pictures—the hummingbirds dancing in a honeysuckle sky... and the stars falling down." He took a sip. "In answer to your question, yes, I remember the day we wrote it. It was one of the best days of my whole life. You had such a way with words and it was easy to put them to music. And you sang like an angel." He shook his head slowly. "And that was the day I..."

"The day you asked me to marry you."

Josie remembered...

It was a week after they met. She had been spending a lot of time with Wes. Not intimate time, just being together time. This day they had gone for a long drive. It was another beautiful Texas evening. About twenty miles out of town, they pulled off the road down a barely visible track that led out onto the prairie. Wes drove without speaking until they dipped down into a hollow you couldn't see from the road. A lazy creek meandered through the wash and a few small cottonwoods stood by the water. Still-green bluestem grass carpeted the area. There was a fire ring and a rough picnic bench. It was a magical spot in the middle of a sun-blasted landscape.

Wes pulled the truck up, and they sat for a moment.

Josie stared out the window. "How did you find this place?"

Wes grinned. "I get around," was all he said.

Josie looked down. "Am I the first girl you ever brought here?" She snuck a glance at his face. It had reddened a bit, so she waited for him to lie to her.

He took a breath. "No, you're not. But you are the first girl I brought here that I ever cared about."

She looked away.

Got out of that one...

"Come on, Josie. Let's sit out for a while."

Wes climbed out, reached behind the seat of the truck, and pulled out his guitar. "There's a blanket and a bag of sandwiches behind your side."

She looked, and to her surprise, there was. She grabbed them, wondering what he had in mind with the blanket.

He took the guitar over to the picnic table and laid it down. Then he went to the bed of the truck. There was a cooler. He brought it over and set it by the bench.

"Got some pop and some cold brewskis, if you like beer."

"I'll stick with the soda, thanks."

He spread the blanket out in the grass. Then he grabbed the bag of sandwiches. "I got baloney and cheese and lunchmeat and cheese and cheese and cheese." He grinned again. "What'll it be?"

She grinned. "Don't you have anything with cheese?"

He laughed. "Well, let me see." He fished around in the bag. "How about..." he pulled a sandwich out with a flourish... "cheese?"

"Well, okay."

"Cheese it is then."

He handed her the sandwich and rustled around in the bag again. He finally pulled one out and squinted at it. "I think I'll have one with cheese in it."

They both laughed. Josie felt comfortable, safe. He grabbed a Coke out of the cooler, handed it to her, and took a Bud for himself. They sat quietly, enjoying the spot, the coolness of the coming evening. With a flash of deep color, a Purple Martin settled on a limb above their heads. He trilled a short song, hopped to another branch, and trilled again.

Wes pulled a piece of bread from his sandwich. "Maybe he's looking for some cheese, too." He flipped the bread out into the grass. The Martin darted down, grabbed the bread, and flew back up into the tree.

Josie watched. "He's been here before, begging handouts. You can tell."

They ate in silence. They watched the sky take on the rosy pink and deeper purples of approaching night.

Wes looked up. "It's a honeysuckle sky, Josie."

"You remembered."

"I wrote it down so I wouldn't forget."

He pulled out the little notepad from his pocket. "Let's write a song, Josie. It'll be our first together."

"I've never done that."

"I can tell you're a natural. You probably sing good, too."

She blushed and looked down. "Well, I sang in church until I quit going. They even let me do a special once in a while, but I..."

"What?"

She thought about church, moved on. "Oh, nothin'." She smiled at him. "Sure, I'd like to try."

He stood, went to the table, and opened the guitar case. She watched him. A little shock ran through her as she followed the way he walked, the way he moved. Like a cat. There was power in him, strength. Nothing wasted in his movements. He took out the guitar and played a chord. It was a little out of tune. He plucked the E string and turned the tuning peg. In a minute, he had it ready. He played a few chords to test, then came and sat beside her.

"I was thinking of something like this." He started a progression and sang the words he had written, the words that had flowed out of her heart that magical night. He had a nice, very smooth baritone voice. She could tell he would probably develop into a bass.

Like Jim Reeves.

"When the hummingbirds danced in a honeysuckle sky and

the stars fell down on the fourth of July..." It was a nice melody, simple but with movement.

He looked at her and his eyes were burning. She had seen him look at her that way the night they met, the night she knew she was going to marry him...

He played the first two lines again and looked at her again. "What's next?"

Suddenly she was terribly afraid... afraid of what was happening in her, to her. She wanted him to touch her, to hold her as tight as he could, but something in her pushed back.

I don't want anyone to touch me. I don't want to love anyone... I...

"I see you got something. Give me the next line."

She looked down. "I can't."

"Come on, sweetheart, just say it. It's like falling off a rock. Easy."

Quietly, almost in a whisper... "She never knew about love 'til she saw it in his eyes."

He nodded. "Sing it."

She looked up. "I... I... oh, Wes, this is hard."

"Sing what you're feeling, Josie, it'll come out easy."

He strummed the chords and sang the first two lines, and then, to her great surprise, she looked straight at him and sang her line. Her voice was rich, somewhere between a second soprano and an alto, and it carried across the clearing like a cool breeze. He stopped and looked at her, this time with awe in his eyes. "Wow. Sing that again, honey."

It was the first time he had called her honey, and it was as though he had found her in some second-hand store, seen the treasure in her, claimed her, redeemed her. They started again. This time together.

"When the hummingbirds danced in the honeysuckle sky
And the stars fell down on the fourth of July
She never knew about love 'til she saw it in his eyes

When the hummingbirds danced in a honeysuckle sky."

He let her take the lead, and he slipped into an easy harmony. Beautiful, smooth. They sang it again.

He smiled, a half-smile, one that made him look like a man instead of a kid. "Okay, we need a couple of verses."

"It's about us, right?"

He nodded. "Yeah, us. You and me."

She looked at him, thought about him, and just said it. "He was a buckaroo cowboy with a dollar in his pocket…."

He picked it right up. "She was a little-town girl with an old silver locket…

They stopped.

He looked at her that way again. "Have I told you I love you yet, Josie?"

She felt the blush coming all the way up her neck. Her head went down, and she looked at the grass. "No."

He put the guitar down and took her hand. "I love you, Josie. I love you and I have since the day I met you." He looked away. "There, I said it."

She felt his hand pulling her to him. She was afraid. Shy. But, yes, he loved her and that was enough. Somebody loved her. She moved closer to him and then… she couldn't.

"She never knew about love, 'til she saw it in his eyes…"

He finished it singing. "When the hummingbirds danced in a honeysuckle sky."

He picked up the guitar again and kept going. "There's nothing like love when it comes like a twister."

Her line. "She was so sweet he couldn't resist her."

They both laughed. He nodded. "You got that right, darlin'."

He paused, took a breath, then… "A man makes a promise, a woman says yes,"

It just came out. "Now she's a wife named Josie with a hubby called Wes."

Something twisted in her. Fear, all the years, the wrongs, the hurt. She lowered her eyes. "I'm sorry, Wes. I don't know why I said that."

He put the guitar down. He moved over and got on his knees. "Is that what you want, Josie?"

She looked into his eyes and saw genuine love. Not lust, not some smirking jerk reaching for her, but a man. A man who cared. She couldn't say yes, she just nodded.

He reached into his pocket. Then there was a small, velvet-covered box. He opened it. A flash of light in the dying sunset. A little diamond in a gold band. "I went out and bought it the next morning. I had to wait for the man to open the store." He took it out of the box. "Will you then?"

She could hardly breathe. "What, Wes?"

"Will you have a hubby named Wes?"

"Are you, are you asking me..."

He nodded. "I love you, Josie. Have from the moment I saw you in the horse barn. I want you to marry me."

"When?"

"Tomorrow if you'll have me."

She nodded again. "Okay. But I think maybe next week. We have to get a license. I need a dress."

"Do you want to get married in a church?"

"No! No church!"

He was surprised at the steel in her reply. "Okay, Josie, whatever you want."

"The courthouse is fine."

He reached for her but she twisted away. "Wait, Wes. I want to make sure. When I hear you promise, then I will belong to you forever. Then you can have all of me."

"Okay. Whatever you want."

He picked up the guitar. The words just tumbled out. "Sweet dreams and colors in the sky. Will you still be with me when the hummingbirds fly? I'm counting on you baby, cause I can't let go…" He paused.

She finished it. "Just keep loving me, please keep loving me, tell me that you love me and we'll never say goodbye…"

Chapter Eleven

THE WAY WE WERE... THE WAY WE ARE

nd that was how they wrote the song. It was as though they made a covenant with very simple conditions. He said, "I love you with all my heart," and she said, "I promise to always stay." And there it was. Josie and Wes. A buckaroo cowboy and a little town girl. She with all her fears and hurts, foolishly trusting him to always be gentle, him with no understanding what being a man really demanded of him... they stepped out on the road to paradise.

And fell in the ditch.

They were married at city hall. She bought a dress at Penny's. It wasn't white because she didn't feel like she deserved a white dress. Instead, she bought a light blue simple cut sleeveless pullover with a bow in the front. It was nice, and it didn't broadcast any messages. He wore a white cowboy shirt with pearl buttons and clean blue jeans. He took a lot of time shining his boots and they looked nice. When the time came, he brought out a tungsten yellow gold band. She had one too. The Judge asked them if they did and they did. And that was that.

When Wes wanted to make love, she didn't know what to do.

He was very gentle, but the first few times he reached for her in bed, she froze. All she could see was Ted, looming over her, the vulgar look on his face, the lies dripping from his mouth, the calloused hands touching her...

She could tell Wes was hurt, but when she tried to tell him the truth, shame gripped her throat like a steel hand. Finally, he said something.

He had rolled away from her when she stiffened under his touch. "I thought you loved me, Josie." His voice was muffled, but she could hear the edge.

She took a deep breath. "I do, Wes. Oh, I do. It's just..." She reached out and touched him gently on his back. He heard the little catch in her throat.

"What is it, honey?"

She felt safer when he called her that. She sat up in bed and looked at him, lying there in a fetal position, turned away. Another deep breath, and then...

"My stepfather molested me."

Wes rolled over, his mouth open. "What? Ted, the guy who was a deacon at the church?"

"Him, yes."

Wes sat up. "I mean, was he... did he....?"

She nodded. She felt the hard place, the scar. She wanted it to break, to crack, to dissolve, but it didn't.

I thought the truth would set you free.

"He started coming into my bed at night when I was thirteen. He said if I told anyone, they would put him in jail and my mother would be out on the street and I would have to go to a foster home. I didn't know what to do."

"He was doing it for four years?"

"Yes."

"What about your mom?"

"She knew all about it."

Wes stood up. "What?"

"Yes. Ted told her he would leave her if she said anything... throw her out on the street. It was his house, his money. My mother had nothing when she married him. So, she just kept her mouth shut and started drinking. And that's why I... why it's hard for me. I want to be your wife, Wes, and I will if you just give me a little more time..."

Wes was angry, but she didn't know if it was at her, or at Ted. He paced beside the bed, turned to her, almost shouted. "You should have told me before we... before I... oh shoot, Josie, this is awful."

She looked at him for a long time and then she just said it. "Awful for me, or awful for you?"

His face reddened. "...For you... of course."

But the brief pause betrayed him.

She turned away. "Do what you want with me, Wes. I'll try to be there too."

She remembered nothing was truly good after that...

THE NEXT MORNING, the day after they talked about the song, Josie just wanted to stay in bed. She didn't want to talk to Wes about anything anymore, not a thing. She didn't want to remember anything, not the songs they wrote, not the marriage going south, not the child they shared, not the hurt, nor the empty years...

He's the one that left me, did me dirt. I don't have to say a word...

Confession is good for the soul...

Josie peeked out from under the covers. Nobody was in the room but her.

I'm losing my hair and now I'm hearing voices. Oh, not to mention I'm going to be dead in five months...

She threw the covers back and swung her legs over the side of the bed. It was cold in the room and once she was out, she moved quickly.

Hope there's a fire...

There was. And the smell of bacon from the kitchen.

They had not talked any more that morning, even though she had promised Wes.

He doesn't keep promises, why should I?

Instead, they had breakfast, coffee, and did some chores. She felt up to that, and Salty was glad to see her. They worked together silently and then Wes suggested they drive out toward Steen Mountain. A Chinook had come through the day before and melted off the snow. There was still some out on the prairie, not much, but enough to put a white frosting on the land and the mountain range ahead. Now it was cold again, a freezing, early winter morning.

She sat wordlessly beside him in the truck, looking out the window. Her breath frosted the glass.

Finally, he spoke. "I hurt you terribly, didn't I?"

She didn't turn her head but kept looking at the frost patterns her breath made on the window. Larger on the out, smaller on the in. "What do you mean?"

"When you told me about Ted. The way I... the way I responded to you."

"That's an old story, Wes. I don't really want to talk about it again. Ted did what he did and you couldn't handle it. Put a fork in it, it's done."

"I should have killed him."

Suddenly rage came up in her throat... bile... and she twisted in her seat like a cat, her fists raised and clenched. The scream tore out of her. "Yes! Yes! Yes! You should have gone over there and beat him and beat him and beat him, crushed his face until he couldn't see, kicked him until all his bones were broken, until he was a mass of blood and butchered flesh... and then you should have dragged him outside and put a bullet between his damn pig eyes."

She saw the sadness in his eyes, the pain on his face. Then the rage drained away, and she was sitting there empty... her face wet with tears. The scar on her heart was still there. Nothing had changed.

"But you didn't, Wes." She turned back to the window. The frosty breath again. "You didn't." Almost a whisper to herself.

Wes was quiet for a long time. The truck purred, the tires clicking on the concrete seams in the old road, buzzing when they hit a macadam patch.

Josie started talking to the window. "I had this all boxed up, Wes. All neatly put away in a sealed-off place in my heart. I didn't think about it, worry about it, try to drink it away. I moved on. My life was not great, but I was making it through. Then you show up and everything is a shitshow. I don't want to feel this. I don't want to remember. I wanted that Josie to be dead."

She took a breath and sighed. The frost went way up the glass. "I think I wished too hard. I killed that one and this one, too."

Josie saw a road sign, green and white. Frenchglen—4 Miles.

In a few minutes, the tiny town came into view. Wes pulled up in front of the Frenchglen Hotel, right in downtown. He put his hand gently on her shoulder and she was too burned out to twist away.

Softly. "Come on. Let's get some lunch. You'll feel better."

They walked into the restaurant area of the hotel. It wasn't luxurious, by any means, but it smelled good. The coffee urn sat between the door to the lobby and the guest bathroom on an oak table. Above the urn hung a rack of cups with the hotel logo. A matronly lady came in from the lobby and waved around the empty room. "Pick a table, folks." She pointed to the urn and the cups. "Help yourself, cream's next to the urn. I'll be with you in a minute."

They got coffee and picked a table. The tablecloth was vinyl, covered with big squares, pink, yellow, orange patterned. There were plates already set—white china with a purple floral design around the edge, a little brown bowl filled with butter packages, salt and pepper shakers. A knife, spoon and fork, and a paper napkin finished the place setting.

The waitress came over with two tall tumblers of water.

Josie looked up. "Can I get a lemon wedge for my water, please?"

"Sure thing, hon."

She ambled away. Josie glanced quickly at Wes. His eyes bored into her and she looked away. There were pictures on the wall and she focused on them. Local shots, the mountain, cowboys. She didn't want to think about Wes, or Ted, or her life, or anything. She felt so full of everything she wanted to vomit it all up. The waitress came back with a couple of slices of lemon on a small plate. Josie squeezed one into the water and took a long drink. The sourness settled.

Wes reached over and took her hand. She tried to pull away, but he held her, strong. "I think if we can get through this, we might be okay."

"What do you mean we, Kemo Sabe?"

He smiled. The smile that made him seem so manly. "Look, Josie. Both of us, we're broken. We need to get better. And if I just rode off into the sunset and left you here…"

"Like you did before?"

He looked away.

"Right now, if you did, I'd die happy." She paused and thought about it. "Or just die."

He shook his head. "We need to get through it. This thing, this scar on both our hearts, I think it can be healed."

She toyed with her fork. What she really wanted to do was get up and run; run out the door, out of her life, out of this world… but she sat.

"What I said in the car, Wes? I meant it. I was doing fine. You showed up and now I'm not."

"I think if we can talk it through, Josie. If I tell you what happened to me and you tell me all about you. We could start back there and make the journey to here, now."

She shook her head. "I don't think you want to hear all about me, Wes. It's the story of a woman who doesn't care. Doesn't care where she goes, doesn't care who she sleeps with, doesn't care how she gets her money. It's a life that means nothing. It started when you left and it never got better. At first, I hated you for it, and then after a while I was just walking through the big numb. Day to day, night by night. No feelings, no love, no dreams… And you know what, Wes? You can't fix it. Josie… she's done."

Wes put his hand over his eyes. "Marry me, Josie."

An electric shock ran through her. She shook her head and stared at him. "What?"

He looked straight at her. "Marry me. I love you, always have. The day I left, I left something there in Texas. I never got it back. I promised you and I broke my word. I've been living on deficit spending ever since."

"You must be out of your freaking mind."

"No, Josie, I'm dead serious."

She stared at him for a long time. Then she realized something. He was the most beautiful man she had ever seen. She covered the realization with a barb. "Who you trying to help, Wesley? Me? Or you?"

"Both of us, Josie. We've both been dead all these years. We need to live again."

She stood up and leaned over the table, palms down. She was talking low. "Don't you remember, Wes? I'm a walking dead woman. Nothing matters because I'm going to be dead in five months. How are you going to make up for all the pain before I die?"

"By just loving you, Josie. Loving you, like only I can love you."

"You hold yourself in pretty high esteem, cowboy." She looked around. The waitress was staring. "Take me home, Wes. I don't want to do this."

They drove all the way back to Burns without a word.

My dad told me later there was a point he and my mom reached, on that winter day out there on the prairie under the Steen Mountains, where it seemed there was nowhere else to go for Wes and Josie. When he asked her to marry him in the restaurant in Frenchglen, she froze up like a deer in the headlights. She made him take her home. Told him she wanted him to leave. And in a way, I don't blame her. After all, he was the one who dumped her. He was the one with a handful of gimme and a mouth full of much obliged. Or so it seemed. But when Wes got back in touch with me and we worked out our stuff, I discovered something about my dad. He really loved her. He really loved Josie. So, he didn't quit this time. He went for the gold. And in doing that, he changed my mama's life, and mine.

Mama. Funny, I didn't call her that until after she died. And with my dad's help, I could find the same peace I think she found. But let me tell you the rest...

Margi.

Chapter Twelve

THE LONG AND WINDING ROAD

Josie waited until the truck pulled up in front of the house. She scrambled out and headed for the house. Then she stopped, turned, and stomped around to Wes's side of the truck. She banged on the glass and he rolled the window down. She leaned in close, almost hissing.

"You need to go away. This is just crazy. I don't know why I ever let you stay."

"Are you sure this time?"

"What do you mean? Of course, I'm sure."

Half smile. The one that drove her crazy. She started to say something, but he interrupted.

"I don't believe you really want me to leave, Josie. And if you just settle down a minute, I'll tell you why."

Josie looked at Wes for a long time, but she saw nothing in his eyes but honesty.

"Okay, what?"

"Can we go inside and talk about it over a cup of hot coffee?"

Another long stare. And again, to her dismay, it occurred to her that Wesley James Branson was the most beautiful man she had ever seen. She looked down at the ground. "Okay."

It was a whisper.

He got out of the truck, took hold of her elbow, and guided her toward the porch. She wanted to jerk away, to scream, to run out into the snow-bound wilderness, keep running until she dropped and then just lie there and freeze to death. She had heard dying of cold wasn't bad, you just kind of went to sleep.

But she didn't... do anything.

He guided her up on the porch and through the door. Steered her into the front room and sat her down. It was cold in the house.

"Give me ten minutes. I'll get a fire going and put the coffee on. In the meantime..." he handed her the afghan quilt from the back of the couch. She wrapped herself in it. He knelt in front of the fireplace. Three small log pieces longways in the hearth, a section of newspaper torn into strips on top of the pieces. Then nine pieces of kindling crosshatched over the paper and another log on top of that longways again. Right out of the Boy Scout Manual. He grabbed a strike-anywhere out of the box and lit the paper. A few helping puffs of breath and the kindling burst into flame. He left it and went into the kitchen. When he came back with the coffee, the kindling was already headed toward coals, so he laid more wood crossways and, in a minute, he had a roaring blaze. He handed her a mug of coffee, the red one, and then sat down. He took a deep breath and then turned to her.

"Did I ever tell you how I learned to ride a bucking horse?"

She stared at him. "What?"

"Did I ever tell you how I learned to ride a bucking horse?"

"No...oo."

What's he up to?

"Bucking is often a symptom of pain somewhere in your horse's body. Anything could cause the pain, anywhere in their body: back, legs, and even an issue where the bit doesn't fit or is irritating your horse's mouth."

"What are you saying?"

"Let me finish."

"After you pinpoint the pain spot, the next thing you need to find out is whether the horse is afraid. Horses are very sensitive prey animals. They are always scanning the surrounding environment, instinctively looking for predators. Any motion near them causes a response in the horse which is a survival mechanism for the prey animal. Anything that moves, regardless of what it is, may cause the horse to start the flight response before an assumed predator approaches. You can be riding along and a leaf blows across the trail and suddenly you are sitting on chain-lightning. So, if your horse is bucking, you need to calm it."

"Another thing I found out was really interesting. Sometimes a horse bucks just because it's lonely."

She stared at him. "What?"

"Yeah, isn't that something? A horse gets left too long by itself and it strikes out at the next person it sees."

"Another reason a horse bucks... it is just flat out being poorly ridden. The rider isn't paying any attention to what the horse needs: They are sitting heavy or they are just confusing the horse because they are not communicating well with the horse and what it needs."

"Why are you saying this...?"

And then the light went on.

"You're talking about me."

Wes nodded, not saying anything.

"I'm not a horse."

"No, you're not. But everything I said is what's happening in your life. You got pain, Josie, genuine pain. In your heart and inside your physical body. And because of what's happened to you, the past and... what's happening to you now, the sickness, you're afraid. And because you've been on your own so long, you're lonely. And to top it off, you've never had someone with a gentle hand."

Josie stood up, fists clenched. "Who made you the freaking

expert on my life? All you ever did for me was take my heart and leave me flat. You never looked back. I hate you, Wesley James Branson. Nothing in my life has ever been the same since you left."

Wes nodded, spread his hands out in a self-deprecating gesture. "I know, Josie, I know, believe me. What you don't know is, it's the same for me. What I did to you has been the greatest sorrow of my life. Don't you see, Josie? I'm not just talking about your life. I'm talking about me too. I've got the same pain, the same fear, and the same aching loneliness. I've been lonely since the day I left."

She stared down at him. "What you said at the restaurant, what you asked me... did you mean it?"

Wes looked at her. A simple answer. "Yes."

"I don't think you did, Wes. And if you did, you are nuts."

"I absolutely meant it, Josie."

"I tell you what, Wes. You are looking at damaged goods. And at this point in my life... well, I'm a woman who has been down every nowhere trail. I'm a liar, and a drunk. I've whored myself, I've stolen, I've taken every drug you can think of and stripped off all my inhibitions when I did. I lived my life full-out in bars and honky-tonks and don't even remember the men I went home with after the show. I've married men I didn't love for their money. I even abandoned my child. I'm the lowest of the low, a slut. Nobody could love me, nobody even likes me."

She stared down at him and took a breath. "Tell you what, Wesley James Branson, I'm going to tell you the entire story and when I finish, what I fully expect is the Wes Branson I know will get on his Brahma Bull and make fast and dusty tracks back to Texas."

Wes smiled the half-smile. "You mean the Wes Branson you knew."

Josie felt the heat rising in her face. "Oohh, you smug... You will, I know you will. The leopard can't change his spots. You can't and I can't. We are who we are. I was damaged goods when you met me and you were a coward. That's the way it was, and that's the way it will stay. As soon as you hear my story, you'll cut and run."

Wes looked up at her and then stood up and it seemed to Josie that it took a long time for him to rise to his full height. When he finally did, he put one hand on her shoulder and lifted her chin with the other until she was looking straight up into his eyes.

"I won't go until you've heard my story too, and then only if you tell me to go and I know you mean it. This is what we said we would do. We would tell each other our story. Well, our agreement was casual before, but now we are gettin' to the place where you pay your money and you take your choice. So, when do we start?"

Josie turned her head away, so she didn't have to look into his burning eyes. "Not today, Wes. I'm done."

"When then, Josie?"

"Tomorrow, I promise."

"Okay. After breakfast tomorrow, we'll start."

THE NEXT MORNING was quiet between them. Wes got up early, built a fire and made breakfast—pancakes with maple syrup, scrambled eggs, plenty of coffee. When they finished, Josie looked across the table.

"How do you want to do this?"

Wes looked down and then said quietly. "I was thinking that we each could take a turn. One person a day so we can really hear what the other one is saying. Then the next day the other person —kinda trade off."

She thought about that for a minute. "That works. Who goes first?"

He reached into his pocket and pulled out a silver dollar. "Call it, the winner chooses." He flipped the coin up, caught it and slapped it hidden onto the back of his free hand.

"Heads."

He uncovered the coin. Kennedy looked sideways out into the future. Wes grinned.

"Your call."

Josie took a deep breath. "I'll go first. That way, I can pop my corn and get it done."

Wes looked out to the front room. "Couch? Coffee?"

She nodded.

He got up and went ahead of her, got her settled, brought a blanket and a cup of coffee, put a log on the fire. She settled in, pulled her knees up, and sat in the corner against the pillow with the blanket around her. She looked around the room. Nothing familiar here except a few pictures she brought from Nevada. Nothing to grab on to, like free-falling off a cliff. She looked over at Wes on the other end of the couch.

"Just do me a favor."

"What?"

"Don't stare at me. Just listen, maybe look at the fireplace. I feel like I'm taking my clothes off in front of somebody for the first time."

"Sure, Josie, whatever you want." He shifted on the couch and put his coffee on the little table between the couch and the fireplace. His eyes followed the dancing flames. "This good?"

She nodded. "Yeah, okay." She took a deep breath and started in. The first words were stiff, kind of stuck in her throat, but then she got going and then she was out and away, in the deep water, opening up her moldy hope chest for all the world to see...

Chapter Thirteen

JOSIE

"*I* didn't think I could go on living the day you left. When I came home after work that night and found the house empty and your stuff gone, I knew right away you'd done a runner. Gone like a cool breeze. Not even a note. I sat down in the middle of the room on the floor. My guts felt like someone had sharpened a four-by-four post and then shoved it right through my diaphragm. It was hard to catch my breath, like I couldn't breathe. I wanted to cry, but I knew I couldn't. So, I screamed. Just once. I didn't want the creepy old lady upstairs calling the cops.

"But you know, looking back, I should have known it would happen. All those promises, all the words, all the lies, the drinking, running around. I should have expected it. After all, I was *el feo,* the ugly one, *bienes dañados,* damaged goods. The things Ted had done to me had ruined me. Ruined me for myself, and ruined me for you. As I sat there, I remembered the look in your eyes when I told you about Ted, what he did to me all those years. The shock and the disgust, then the flush as you realized your eyes had betrayed you.

"So, there it was. Wes and Josie were just a dream and our life evaporated like the morning mist on desert sand at sunrise. I sat there for an hour in the middle of the floor, my head down, my guts aching... and then I remembered Margi. I got up and called my sitter. Apologized for being so late. Asked if Margi could stay overnight. Geraldine was good with that. I got up and went to the window. The sun was already down and it was that semi-dark outside where the day-world starts to disappear. Cars went down the street with lights already on and I could hear the jukebox from Pepe's Can-Do club down the street. Under the streetlight on the corner, the neighborhood hooker plied her trade. Maybe I wasn't in hell, but I could see hell from my window.

"I had an idea. I went into the kitchen. If you could call it a kitchen with its tiny stove and sink, a little refrigerator on one wall of the room and one of those green-topped aluminum dinette sets against the other. I pulled one of the vinyl covered chairs over to the counter, climbed up and started looking through the cupboards. In a few minutes, at the back of the top shelf above the stove, I found what I was looking for—an almost-full bottle of Villa One Silver Tequila you had somehow missed. Your favorite for making margaritas. I got it down and went back to my spot on the floor. I took a big swig, sat for a minute, and then nearly threw up. It was awful. But... then I felt a subtle warmth steal into my face. I took another swig. Not so bad this time. A little warmer in my gut. A kind of peace. I tipped it up and took a long swallow and then sat with it. Better now. The pain was losing its knife edge. I liked it. Maybe this was the way out of this grinding ache I was feeling, an ache like a tooth under a slow dentist drill without the Novocain.

"I didn't know what to do. I took another swig and another... and sat for a long time, feeling the heat come on me. And then, like I got kicked in the head by a horse, it hit me.

"I didn't need you!

"I could get through this. I had survived Ted abusing me; I had survived my mother abandoning me; I had survived giving birth, and I could survive Wesley James Branson, for goodness' sake. I wasn't gonna just sit there and die.

Think! Make a plan. Get moving.

"The thoughts came unbidden, like someone was standing over my shoulder and pushing me into action. I got up and went to the phone. I called my boss at the nightclub. He answered, and I knew he was behind the bar. I could hear the customers, laughing, slurred loud voices, the clink of glasses. The band was playing and he had to speak up.

"This is Denny."

"Hi Denny, this is Josie."

"Hey, baby, what's going on?"

I just got to the point. "I got a big problem."

I could hear the concern in his voice. "What's up?"

"Wes left me. He just took off and now I'm kinda stranded here and I wanted to ask a favor."

"Sure, baby, what can I do for you?" Now I heard the opportunity knocking in his voice.

"I need to borrow some money until I get back on my feet."

There was a pause. Then, "How much do you need?"

"A few hundred, just until I get going on my own. I'll pay you back, I promise."

Now I could almost see him looking around, thinking. "Well, I don't know, Josie…"

I just laid it on the table. I was thinking about the times he had come on to me, pressing up against me in the back room, touching me. I knew how to make this work. "Look, Denny, you like me, don't you?"

"Why sure, honey."

"If you help me, I'll be very nice to you."

"A pause. I could almost hear his thoughts turning over in his head. Thinking about what I had just said, thinking about his wife…

"Do you mean…?"

"Yes, Denny, that's exactly what I mean."

"But how...?"

"I'm alone now, Denny, on my own. No Wes to bother you. If you want to be discreet, we can meet here at my place, just you and me. Just let me know when you're coming so I can get Margi to a sitter."

And that was that. My first step down the long and winding road.

Josie stared at the fire. She had told her story almost in a whisper. Now she took another breath and went on.

"AFTER THAT, I did what I had to do. Denny was the first stop on a long bus ride. A string of men who thought they were using me, but, truth to tell, I was the one doing the using. Denny made me sick, but he gave me the money I needed, and so did all the rest of them.

"I bided my time and kept looking and after a while I found a better job in a better bar. The drill was the same. Use my feminine wiles to get what I needed. The owner was a self-made "respectable" citizen named Bobby Payton, who owned three restaurants in Laredo. Pulling him in was easy. After I had been in his bed for a while, he made me head cashier. I figured out how to skim the till. That lasted almost a year. He caught me dipping, but the pictures I had taken of him in my bed passed out, the ones I promised to send to his wife and kids, convinced him he should just let me go. I walked away with thirty thousand. I even got a good reference from him.

"The best part of that time early on after you left was when a guy at Ted's church caught Ted molesting his little daughter in the church basement. The father beat him so bad Ted had a heart attack and died a few hours later. The little girl's dad didn't even see the inside of a jail because it was Texas and that's what they do to pervs. So, Ted was dead, and I was never happier. The only thing that would have made me happier was if I had been there to watch the beating.

"I waited six or seven months and then I went to see my mother. She had a religious experience after Ted departed and she was stone cold sober and very repentant. She begged me to forgive her. I liked that part. Then she tried to convert me and I told her where to go. When she was running Bible verses by me, I asked her casually if she thought Ted was roasting in hell and how did she think he felt and that shut her up. But I wasn't too hard on her because she really wanted to spend time with Margi and she didn't charge me anything for babysitting. I could leave Margi there for long weekends, which opened a whole new life for me.

"Free and easy, no one to be responsible to, my mom taking Margi more often. After about two years, I got a great job at a country bar downtown. I was a waitress, but I started hanging with the guys in the band after hours. One night when I was drunk, I came up and sang with the band during their show. I guess I did good because the place went wild and the bandleader, a piano guy who played a lot like Floyd Cramer, asked me to sing with the band. I remembered what you taught me about singing, how to extend my range. I spent a lot of time learning Loretta Lynn, Patsy Cline, Skeeter Davis, and my very favorite, Tammy Wynette. I used to get a real kick out of standing up their singing 'Stand By Your Man'. The band could never figure out why I laughed at the end of the song.

"The tough part about singing in a country band was the rodeo studs hittin' on me after every show. I could smell them a mile away. Rodeo wannabes. They may as well have worn their chaps and spurs into the bar. They all wanted to get next to the little lady with the great big voice. They were such fools. Just like you, Wes. They thought the world revolved around them just because they could stay on a bull for eight seconds. WowWee! That's certainly worth a lifetime of living. So, all I needed to do to get what I wanted was to tell them what they wanted to hear. You know all about that, don't you, Wes? A pushy blonde with a big chest and off you go. Well, don't frown, Wes Branson... I learned it from you.

"And that's how I became a country singer in a country band. I slipped right into it, and, to my surprise, I was pretty good. I started making a lot more singing than I did waitressing, but Gary, the piano player, showed me there was a lot more to the music business than just standing behind a microphone, so I improved myself. I bought a nice Gibson Hummingbird guitar and learned to play. I found out that anybody with even a lick of talent can do it if they stay with it. Just like riding a bull. Stay with it. After a year of hard work, my chops were pretty solid, to where I could play and sing on my own. Then I remembered when we wrote Hummingbirds and my world expanded. I figured if I wrote one good song, I could write another and after I brought a few in, the band started playing my songs. I didn't let them do Hummingbirds though. That just would have been too much. So, I kept that song for myself, until I met Tommy Franklin. And that's where I'm stopping today because I am suddenly very tired and very sad."

Josie looked over at Wes. It startled her to see he had put his head down in his hands. When he looked up, his face was wet.

He's tender. He's changed. But...

Wes stood up. "Let me help you." He took two steps and then he was lifting her and she was in his arms as he carried her gently to her room. Her arms stole around his neck and she put her head on his chest and closed her eyes. In that moment, she realized that a tiny piece of the scar that surrounded her heart was gone.

Chapter Fourteen

WES

The next morning came around early, except Josie didn't get up for a long time. The "It" had paid a visit during the wee hours and she was up most of the night dosing the pain. Finally, around five o'clock, she fell into a troubled sleep and she woke about nine with a morphine hangover. She lay in her bed with the covers pulled up to her chin, her eyes half closed. A weak winter sun shone through the window. A shadow passed on the shade. Wes, on his way to the barn. She heard the crunch of his boots in the snow that had piled up on the south side of the house. Then Salty nickered a hungry greeting as the barn door creaked open. A strange feeling of belonging to... something... came over her. She didn't like it.

I'm on my own. I always have been. I don't need him or anyone.

She remembered the feeling she had when she first came to Burns, a feeling so strong she pulled off the road. The day when, for the first time in her life, she knew she might be where she was supposed to be. She remembered her thoughts.

I'm Josie Winters. Before today, I have never been happy, well, except once, a long time ago... but I love my horse. And somehow, I know... I will never leave this place.

She had been right that day for all the wrong reasons.

After a long time, Josie felt the call of nature and she crept out from under the down comforter and swung her feet over the side of the bed. She heard Wes come into the kitchen through the back door.

I was happy once, a long time ago, before he left. Five years... well, four-and-a-half until he started going mean on me. I was only ever happy with Wes. I wasn't happy before; I wasn't happy after.

It suddenly occurred to her she needed to hear his side.

Two sides to every coin, Josie.

She went into the bathroom, then washed her face and brushed her hair. She checked the brush.

Not as many clumps today.

She got herself dressed, put on a sweater against the cold, and went out to the front room. Wes was putting wood in the box by the fireplace. The fire was already going.

"Hey, Jose, how are you today?"

She shook her head. "Tough night. Had a visitor. It took a long time to kill the pain. Now I'm a little hungover."

"Get you some coffee?"

Josie nodded. "That would be good. Sorry, it's so late. You can pass on the narrative today if you want."

Wes smiled. "If you're up for it, I'm good. Breakfast first?"

Josie grimaced. "I'm a little off my feed."

"Oatmeal, yogurt? Something kind to the tummy?"

"You know, oatmeal sounds good. We got any raisins?"

"Just waiting for you to ask." Wes smiled again. "Sit down."

Wes let her slip into her spot in the corner of the couch and handed her the afghan. She wrapped it around her legs, covered her lap, and watched him as he went out to the kitchen. The fire felt good. She heard him run some water, open a cupboard. A pot rattled on the stove.

"Give me ten minutes and I'll have this for you." He came out with a cup of coffee, the red mug. It was hot and bracing, just the right amount of half and half.

He knows me like a country road.

In a few minutes, he brought her a bowl of oatmeal—the raisins plumped up just right and the oats cooked to perfection. He moved the coffee table down and put down a little cream pitcher of half and half.

"Better than milk."

She poured it on and then took a bite.

Good, really good.

Josie felt better. She didn't want to, but she did. She finished the oatmeal quickly.

"More?"

She shook her head.

When am I just going to relax and let this happen?

And then she knew why. She was still afraid. She didn't trust him. There were too many rocks in the river she had come down, too many crash landings, too many waves had swamped the boat.

Why in the world would I trust this guy?

Wes sat down. Looked at the fire, then at her.

"I know you still don't trust me, Josie."

Josie stared at him.

Stay out of my head, Wes.

Then she said it out loud. "You're right, Wes, I don't. I have no reason to trust you. Oh, this is all very comfy. You cooking, takin' out the trash, feeding the horse, lighting the fire. But I needed that when I was eighteen, not when I'm fifty-six. Yes, I need something, but I don't know what it is and I damn well know that you can't give it to me."

Wes shrugged. "Maybe, maybe not. That could be true, but... at this point in your life, are you willing to take a chance that maybe I actually can give you what you need?"

"And what do I need, smart guy? You tell me."

"You need unconditional love."

"What's that supposed to mean?"

"You need someone who loves you for no other reason than just because he does. Someone who expects nothing back, someone who just loves you."

"Is that you, Wes? If it is, how did you go from Mr. Self-centered to Mr. Nice Guy?"

"If you let me tell you what happened to me, maybe you'll find out."

She stared at him for a long time. She didn't want to find out, she didn't want to be here, she didn't want him to be here, she didn't want to... still love him.

She took a deep breath.

"If you tell me and I find out, what happens then?"

"Why don't you just see?"

Another long silence.

"Okay." A whisper.

"When I left Texas, I drove out to California with Veda. We went there because it was the next biggest Rodeo state. Veda was always pushing me to compete, but when we got there, my funds were running low. I needed to go to work. I didn't have the money to pay the entrance fees, and that bugged her. I got a job at a construction company building houses up by Palmdale. We were living in a two-bit motel with one room. It had a kitchenette and a bathroom and a bed. She complained all the time. It lasted about six weeks and then she met another rodeo guy in a bar down the street when I was at work. He bought her a few drinks, talked the talk to her for a few days and one night when I got back to the motel, she was all packed and ready to go. The guy was in an Impala with the engine idling out front. Veda patted me on the arm as she left."

"Oh, Wessy, it was fun, but Jimmy is already on the rodeo.

We're going to Sacramento this weekend to watch him ride. He's gonna be a big star. I like you a lot, but a girl's just got to look out for herself."

"And that was that. When I closed the door behind her, I felt a sense of relief. You know, it was like climbing up on a bronc in the chute, suddenly realizing this would not turn out well, then feeling extremely happy that you were still alive after you picked yourself up out of the dirt in the middle of the arena.

"I got very drunk that night and every night after for a long time. I could barely hold a job, but somehow, I did. I was out of it for a long time—six months, maybe. I was empty inside, but I was too proud to go back to you. So, I just let it slide. I started playing guitar again and one night I sat in with a couple of guys at a bar down the street. We played some Hank Williams, and the folks liked it, so the owner gave us a job. I was making twenty-five a night, three nights a week, plus my pay from the construction job. I was just skating by. It was not good. I had a lot of rage. One night I got really demolished at the bar and went out and smashed out some windows in some stores downtown. The cops picked me up, and they gave me a choice—the hoosegow or the military. They classified me as a "delinquent" since I was only twenty. That meant my behind belonged to the military because of the war. So rather than let them draft me into the army, I joined the marines.

"The next thing I knew I was at Camp Pendleton in the 5th Marine Regiment, Ist Battalion, Ist Marines. That was April. We trained for ten weeks and then they shipped us out. I ended up in Vietnam, still thinking I was a tough guy. I found out different.

"We served in Da Nang, Đông Hà, Con Thien, Quảng Trị, Huế, Phu Bai and Khe Sanh. Basically, they sent us out into the countryside to search and destroy. Go out and find the VC, the Viet Cong, or the NVA, the North Vietnamese regular troops, or both. When we found them, we killed them or they killed us. It was hell. We crawled through leech infested swamps; we crept through impassable jungles on our hands and knees; we climbed hills that were defoliated with Agent Orange and a lot of us got sick. We ghosted through the crop fields; we sat in foxholes filled nearly to the top from the rain. It was hard just to stay alive.

"I made a couple of friends, Steve Connor and Luis Hidalgo. We were Texicans, so we stuck together. They had my back, and I had theirs. The first time I came under fire was very scary. I was on guard in a wooden tower on the front perimeter of our camp. There was small arms and mortar fire coming from the Vietnamese village across the highway. I was by the bunker where you could look down on the fence. Every eighth or ninth round was a tracer round — red or green. When you saw tracers, that meant there were a lot of bullets you didn't see. The tracers started coming over the fence, moving down the line towards where I was standing. They were coming in ten feet above the ground or so. Then Charlie—that's what we called the Viet Cong —started bringing the altitude down. I could hear the bullets coming, like a swarm of angry bees, chest high and angry. I ducked down below the sandbags and peed my pants.

"The worst fight I was in before Tet was near Kien Hoa. They came at us in the night and almost overran us. One guy in our platoon had a little terrier dog. Well, that pup smelled them coming and started barking. Woke us up just in time to fight off the first wave. We fought them for four hours without a letup. The Viet Cong launched four major assaults on our positions. We killed over 300 enemy soldiers. Thankfully, Steve and Luis and I made it through, but fifteen guys in our command did not. Then came Hue. I told you about that. That's where we lost Steve."

Wes stopped and ran his hand over his face. He looked away. Josie saw the tears.

"You can stop, Wes, if you want."

Wes stood up. "Yeah, if you don't mind. I need to pull myself together. This is a lot harder than I thought. I know it's your turn, but let me pick up tomorrow when I've pulled myself together. I told you about Steve, and how I got my scarred face, but I didn't tell you the entire story. Is that okay?"

And then Josie felt something for Wes she never thought she'd feel for anyone.

Compassion.

Chapter Fifteen

GONE...

The next morning, Josie was up early. The night had passed uneventfully. After Josie dressed and gussied up a little, she came out. The front room was chilly.

Wes didn't make a fire. Odd.

She went into the kitchen. It was dark. The coffee pot still had some of yesterday's coffee in it and the old grounds were still in the top dispenser. Josie was puzzled. Wes had a routine. He always ground the next morning's coffee and filled the tank in the coffee maker the night before so he could just walk in and turn it on. She went to the mud porch off the kitchen and slipped on her muck boots and a jacket. When she went outside, Wes's truck was gone. Her heart did a little jump.

What if he left?

She ran around to the back of the house. The trailer was there beside the barn. She didn't like the feeling of relief that came over her. She fought it.

What if he left? Who cares? He doesn't owe me anything and I certainly don't need him.

But then it hit her. She did need him. She needed him more than she had ever needed anyone in her life. Josie Winters was riding down a trail that led to darkness, the end, nothingness, and Wes Branson showed up to ride that trail with her, the only one who came to help. And she knew in the months or weeks left to her she would need him desperately. And in that moment, she felt something breaking, something that had pinned her to the wall for so many years she'd lost count. She needed Wes, and it didn't matter if she could trust him, or if he didn't stay the course, it just didn't matter. She needed him and she would take what she could get.

Josie sat inside the whole day, wrapped in a blanket. The house had a furnace, but it didn't really keep anything warm, so she just piled as many blankets on as she could and dozed on the couch. She had to get up a couple of times to take her meds and use the bathroom, but mostly she just sat staring, waiting...

The sun moved toward the west and it was growing dark in the house when she finally heard his truck pull into the driveway. She threw off the blankets, lept to her feet, and ran to the door. She had not bothered to turn on any lights, so shadows filled the room. As she stood there in the dark, she was trembling. Part of her wanted to smash him, scream at him, kick and yell, accuse, but she knew she wouldn't.

You don't care about that anymore, Josie. You just need him. You're afraid and alone and he's here, and he's changed...

She backed away from the door. She heard his footsteps across the gravel and then he came up on the porch. Her heart was pounding. She felt him try the door and then he stopped. Maybe he was turning away...

Don't go, Wes.

Then the door handle turned, and the door swung open. She could see the outline of his broad shoulders in the last dying light from the sun. He spoke.

"Josie?"

And then she was running to him and she was in his arms.

"Wes, oh, Wes! I thought you left."

She felt his arms come around her and then he was holding her so tight she couldn't breathe.

"Wes, Wes, please, oh, Wes, please..."

"Josie, my darling girl, Josie, Josie."

She wanted to get closer to him, to bury herself in him, to lose everything of her into him, but she couldn't. She couldn't because he was already holding her as tight as he could. And she was crying, crying like she'd never cried in her life. Sobbing, gasping. And Wes was kissing her face, and her eyes, and her lips and her cheeks.

"Oh Josie, I'm so sorry. I'm so sorry for how I hurt you. Please, forgive me."

Somewhere in the back of her mind, the word "forgive" started creeping around like a lizard crawling on a hot rock. Forgive. It was a word that brought pictures of people that did terrible things to you and then tried to get off the hook by asking you to 'forgive' them. She slowly stopped her crying. Wes was still holding her, but she had stiffened.

"What, Josie."

She whispered in his ear. "I don't like that word, Wes. It's everybody's easy way out. Besides, I haven't ever forgiven anyone in my life and I don't know how."

"What do you want, Josie?"

"I just want to stay in this safe place I'm in. The place of knowing I need you, but not trusting you to stay. That's what works right now. I'm not ready to forgive anything. Maybe I won't ever be."

He was silent for a moment. Then he sighed. "Okay. But maybe, after we talk this all out, you might see that forgiveness, real forgiveness, can heal a lot of diseases."

"It won't heal this cancer."

Wes pulled his head back and looked at her. "No, you're right. It probably won't. But it will make the road end easier."

"You seem pretty sure."

He nodded his head. "Josie, I've been a lot of places and down a lot of trails since I abandoned you. I've needed forgiveness and I've also learned to forgive in these last thirty years. I've gotten a lot of my mistakes sorted out and I'm riding easy with them. But not with you. Because you did nothing to me, I was the one. It was me who did the damage, me who caused the hurt, it was all me. That's something that, unless I go back to drinking and just stay in a fog for the rest of my life so I can shut it out of my mind and my heart, I will always live with, something that will always gnaw at me, and I must make right. And that's why I'm here. I have to make it right somehow... I hope and pray that you will let me."

She realized she was still in his arms. Suddenly, before she even thought about it, there were words coming out of her mouth. "Wes, will you make love to me, please?"

He looked back, way deep into her eyes, and this time she saw the sadness behind the half-smile that always drove her crazy. "Only if you marry me, Josie. Only if you marry me."

***

IT WAS NIGHT, late. The fire was going, and the room was finally warm. Wes had fixed her a nice dinner, some chicken in mushroom sauce over rice. He had some ice water with his and she had some white wine. After the main course, he brought out a blackberry pie, cut two pieces, and warmed them in the toaster oven. Then he spooned some vanilla ice cream on top.

"Where did you get all this stuff?"

Wes only smiled. "I don't spend every minute in my trailer. I get out-and-about some days."

"So I see. This was a delicious dinner. Where did you learn to cook? When we were married, you couldn't cook a Marie Callender pot pie."

"When I was in the Marines, I was a screw-up for most of my

hitch. I spent a lot of time on KP and I picked up a few things. Sometime I'll have to cook you some Ga kho gung."

"What in the world is that?"

"Vietnamese ginger chicken."

"I bet that's an interesting story."

"What?"

"How you learned to make… what was it?"

He smiled. "Ga kho gung. Yeah, I guess I'll tell you that story too."

He cleaned up the dishes. It was late.

"Wes, where did you go last night? What happened to you?"

He stood at the sink looking out the window, drying the last plate. She came and stood beside him. Moved in close. He put down the dish towel, put his arm around her and she moved up tight, as close as she could. She put both her arms around his waist. Encircled him, held him. He was so real, so strong. She never wanted to leave. It was safe here, at least for now.

Wes. Wes…

The moon was out, and it was obviously cold outside because there was a frost on the ground and the moonlight glinted off the land with a cold brilliance. She looked up at him.

"Tell me?"

He sighed, then nodded, took hold of her shoulders, and turned her toward the front room. They went in and he got her comfy in her spot. The fire had died down and there was a bed of coals. He threw on a couple more pieces of pine. It was quiet, and they sat for a while. Then Wes turned to Josie.

"I told you I had two friends, Steve Connor and Luis Hidalgo. I guess I didn't really make myself clear. We were more than friends, we were brothers. There's something that happens in war that someone who has not been there will never understand. You figure out after you been through hell with your buddies, after you've pulled their butts out of the fire and had yours pulled out… well, you figure out you are not fighting for democracy, or the good ol' USA or Mom, the flag, and apple pie. You're fighting, with all your strength and all your skill, to keep yourself and your buddies alive. When I talked about Steve dying the other day..." Wes paused and looked back at the coals. "I didn't know how hard it would hit me. I stayed up after you went to bed and then it all just crashed down on me. I was back in Hüe, back with Steve and Luis in the middle of that battle. It was so real, I had to get out. Got in my truck and just headed down the highway. It was about eleven. I didn't know where I was going, so I just drove for about two hours until I came to a little town. Vale, the sign said. I came into town on the main street and there was a bar and barbecue open, the Sagebrush Saloon. I parked and went in. I wanted to get drunk, really drunk."

Josie looked at Wes with wide eyes. He shook his head.

"Yeah, Josie, I know. I don't drink. But I tell you I had a powerful thirst. I wanted to belly up to that bar and look on red likker until I blacked out. I walked up and ordered a double. The barkeep brought it and I stood there for a long time staring at it. Finally, the bartender came over.

"You a vet?"

"Yeah, how'd you know?"

"You got the thousand-yard stare. I seen it a lot. And you've got a love-hate relationship with that double in front of you. You want to drink it down and order up another, but you don't dare."

He wiped the bar down with a bar cloth that was hanging over his shoulder.

"Nam?"

I nodded. "Yeah."

"Been having flashbacks?"

Nodded again. "Yeah, bad. Open-eyed."

"Marines."

"Yeah, 1st Marines."

"Semper fi, Mac, I'm 7th."

"Chu Lai?"

"Yep, first blood, 1965. You guys were at Hüe, later on. That was a tough one. Lose buddies there?"

"Yeah, the best."

"Wanna talk about it?"

Wes turned to Josie. "So, I sat there until four o'clock, spilling my guts. Gordy, the bartender, ran everybody out at two, made me some coffee and warmed up some ribs from the Barbecue side of his establishment. We talked a long time. I told him about Steve. It was the first time I ever really talked about it. When it got really late, he shut the place up, took me to his house, made up a bed on the couch and I crashed there. We both got up late and Gordy made me breakfast. We went out for a drive and talked some more."

Josie shifted a little under her blankets. "Did you tell him about me?"

"Yeah, Josie, I did."

"Did it help? I mean to talk about your friend?"

Wes nodded. "Yes. Surprisingly, it did."

"Will you tell me?"

"Yes, honey, I'll tell you. In the morning."

Josie nodded.

He called me honey.

Chapter Sixteen

TET

The next morning, they had breakfast and coffee. Wes got Josie comfy in front of the fire, went out and fed Salty, and then came back with the pot. He poured them both a mug and then sat at the other end of the couch. Josie patted the spot by her. "Sit here, Wes."

He scooted over and put his hand on her leg. She felt the weight of it like a rock; big, strong, warm.

He always had warm hands.

He sighed. "Ready?"

She nodded.

As I'll ever be.

He put his mug down. "I should probably give you a little background, so here goes. I didn't know much when I went out there, but after I got home, I read a lot about Vietnam. The history, how we got involved—the whole deal was a real boondoggle. Here's what happened."

"At the end of World War II, the allies had liberated all of Southeast Asia. But the Vietnamese monarchy had collapsed, and the Japanese decimated the country before they left. A young Vietnamese man who was western educated and desperately wanted democracy for his country came to the allied commanders and asked them to help him rebuild Vietnam. His name was Ho Chi Minh. They rejected his proposal and instead they handed Vietnam over to France, who immediately turned it into a French colony and started stripping the resources. Well, that really ticked Ho Chi Minh off and he moved north to Hanoi and turned to communist China for help, which they were more than willing to give. Meanwhile, the French lived like kings in the South and the Vietnamese people lived like slaves.

"With China's help, Ho Chi Minh formed an army and started attacking the French. After some bloody battles, he surrounded and defeated them at Bien Dien Phu, destroying fifteen thousand French troops. The French called desperately for negotiations and eventually they agreed in Geneva to partition the country along the 17th parallel, with the North governed by Ho Chi Minh and the south led by a so-called pro-democratic government that the French installed before they left. That was in 1954. The agreement said there would be democratic elections in 1956 to reunite the country, but that never happened. So, Ho Chi Minh started another war to unify the entire country, but now instead of democracy, he was going to model it after the Soviet and Chinese regimes. He trained an army of guerillas, the Viet Cong, and began sending them into the South. Meanwhile, the US Military Assistance Advisor Group took responsibility for training South Vietnamese troops. The first Americans died during a guerrilla strike at Bien Hoa in 1959. Eventually President Kennedy sent one hundred American advisors in 1961. Then, in 1962, American forces started using Agent Orange to defoliate trails used by the Viet Cong. Things went from bad to worse and by 1963, the US government increased the number of advisors and Special Forces to twenty-one thousand troops.

"By then, Kennedy had serious misgivings about our involvement. He told his closest advisors he was going to take us out of the war, but in November he was assassinated and Johnson took over. In 1964, the North allegedly attacked two US destroyers in the Gulf of Tonkin. Congress authorized President Johnson to wage all-out war. And there we were.

"In 1965, our first combat troops arrived, two Marine battalions. We started bombing North Vietnam in 1966 with B-52s. And that's the lead-up to how Wesley James Branson ended up in Southeast Asia."

Wes looked over at Josie. She was staring at him, eyes open wide. He smiled and went on.

"I arrived there in the summer of 1967. I was in the 1st Marines. Steve, Luis, and I fought together through some tough battles. Then, in late 1967, the North Vietnamese got tired of having their behinds kicked all over the South. They figured out that if the Americans kept winning, they would probably invade the North, so they abandoned their guerrilla tactics and came after us. Their commander, Giap, rolled the dice and hoped to come up big. He almost did.

"They massed six infantry divisions near the border with North Vietnam and, in the fall of 1967, started a lot of action— firefights, ambushes, raids—in the north near the DMZ, hoping to draw our troops up there. It worked. In the meantime, the Viet Cong and North Vietnamese Army secretly began a massive buildup of troops in the SUSouth. Then on January 21, 1967, they laid siege to the US Marine combat base at Khe Sanh. We rushed troops there after President Johnson declared we must hold the base at all costs. Ten days later, Giap violated the so-called Tet cease-fire and unleashed 84,000 troops on thirty-six provincial capitals. His plan was to over-run the South Vietnamese army and the US troops. Hüe was the most important city, because it had been the capital of unified Vietnam and meant a lot to Ho Chi Minh. Well, they captured it. The brass sent us over to dig them out. I think I told you this next part.

"We got there February 14th. I was in Delta Company and we spearheaded the counter-attack. After some vicious fighting, we took the Citadel, a fortified section of the old city. Remember, we had been fighting in dense jungles so combat in those tightly packed streets was difficult, if not impossible. The jungle eats up sounds, but in Hüe all that sound ricocheted off the walls. It was ear-splitting. Every corner, every building became perfect sniper nests and ambush points. The bullets, grenades, and artillery were coming at us from every direction.

"After some tough fighting, my company regrouped at Dang Ba Tower. We needed the tower as an observation point, so they told us to charge it, kill all the enemy, and hold it. It seemed simple. But the place was alive with NVA regulars. They were in sniper foxholes and behind rubble. When we were going in, they let us have it. My buddy, Steve Connors, went down with bullets in his legs."

Wes stopped for a minute, took a breath, and went on. "This is the part I didn't tell you. Steve, Luis, and I got separated from the rest of our guys. We ducked into the basement of a bombed-out building. It was just the three of us. We took up positions at the windows and held them off. Then we took an eighty-eight shell right through the window. Blew the place to pieces. Luis, my other buddy, got hit real bad. Steve was bleeding badly, too, so I started to pick him up. He pushed me away. He looked up at me and said. 'Get Luis out of here. I'll give you cover.'

"I argued, but he wouldn't hear it. 'Luis is hit bad. I just got flesh wounds in the legs. Luis is gonna die unless you get him to an aid station. I'm good. You need me to cover you.' And then he looked at me and smiled. 'Wes, you've been a great pard and I've loved riding the river with you. Now git!' Then he said something that stuck with me all these years. He smiled up at me and said. 'Don't worry, I'm not afraid to die.' He had the most peaceful look on his face. Then he turned back to the window and started giving me cover. Last thing I heard was him hollerin' at me. 'Wes! Git!'

"I picked up Luis and dragged him out the back. I got him

into an alley and threw him over my shoulder in a fireman's carry. Then I headed away from the fighting, but I got lost. I wandered around for an hour with Luis on my back before I found an aid station. I got him on a cot and a medic showed up. He looked Luis over, then he looked up and shook his head. 'He's in terrible shape. I gotta get him on a Medevac.' I helped them get Luis onto a Huey. I didn't see him again for ten years. As the helicopter carried him away, I headed on a dead run back for the Tower. When I got there, the fighting had moved off into another sector. It was as quiet as the grave. When I came up the street, there were VC and NVA stacked up in front of our hideout. I counted twenty-five enemy dead. A grenade had blown the door open, so I scrambled over the rubble and into the basement. Steve was sitting up against the wall on the far side of the room. There were five more dead VC in front of him. His rifle was across his lap and his knife was in his hand. He was dead. They had bayoneted him a bunch of times. I checked his rifle and his pack. He had used up all his ammo and was standing them off with his Kay Bar when they killed him. Like Jim Bowie at the Alamo or something. But you know what the strangest thing was, Josie?"

Josie looked over at Wes and shook her head. Tears were streaming down his face. "He still had that smile on his face. He looked so peaceful. He was beautiful. I just stared at him. Then I stumbled out the door. Just as I did, a mass of rocket and mortar fire lit me up. Shrapnel hit me in the face and legs and knocked me out. I woke up in a hospital two days later. After a month, they shipped me stateside. Luis was gone, and I had no idea where he was.

"After they assessed the spot where we held off the enemy, they decided we were heroes. They gave me a medal and awarded one to Steve posthumously. I guess our little salient had prevented the VC from rounding up the rest of the guys in our platoon. But it wasn't me, it was Steve. He gave his life so me and Luis could live. He was the one who defended that spot. It was

Steve who was the real hero. But for a long time, I couldn't figure it out. He wasn't afraid at all and I was scared stiff. He had something that I knew nothing about. I didn't figure out what it was until years later."

Josie was going to ask Wes what it was, what Steve had, but she looked at his face and knew Wes was done. She lifted her arms and Wes came into them. He laid his head on her shoulder and she pulled him close, comforting. She could feel him shaking, holding back the tears. Josie kissed him gently on the cheek. She felt the tears starting in her eyes.

"It's okay, Wes. You can cry for Steve. I'm here. It's okay."

And Wesley James Branson sat with Josie Winters and they both cried. Tears of sorrow, tears that washed the years away, tears that lifted the curtain of the past and opened something in both of their hearts; a way forward, a cleansing, a redeeming of souls, a promise.

Chapter Seventeen

TOMMY FRANKLIN

"*D*id you ever hear of a guitar player named Tommy Franklin?" Josie was sitting across the table at breakfast the next morning.

Wes thought for a moment. "Didn't he play on some hit records outta Nashville?"

"Yeah. A couple."

"What about him?"

"He's part of my story. A part I need to share with you because you are part of it, too."

Wes looked puzzled. "How so? I never met the guy."

"He and I played in a band together. He was my boyfriend..."

Wes looked at Josie with a quizzical grin.

"Okay, he was my lover."

"So, where do I fit in?"

"Okay, it's kind of complicated, but I guess it's my turn for show and tell. Meet you on the couch."

JOSIE TOOK a sip of her coffee. Wes had taken his usual place at the other end of the couch, and that was fine with Josie because she needed plenty of room to open herself up.

"I guess I should start with my band."

Wes grinned. "A band. I knew you could do it."

"Well, it wasn't much until Tommy Franklin joined. We called ourselves the Red Hot Country Mamas. I had another girl with me, Denise. We came off kinda like Linda Ronstadt and Emmy Lou Harris. We were pretty good, but we weren't really going anywhere. Then one night, this tall cool drink of water shows up at a bar where we were playing in Laredo with his guitar and an amp. Asked if he could sit in."

"Tommy Franklin?"

Josie nodded. "Yep, Tommy Franklin. We probably would have shined him on, but it was the third set and the crowd had thinned out so we thought, what the heck, and let him set up his stuff. Well, to our surprise, the boy was chain lightning in a bottle. I mean, he could really play. We started out with that old Wilma Cooper song, 'This Ole House.' Tommy did some picking that made his guitar sound just like a banjo. Folks started perking up around the bar. Then we pulled out 'The Auctioneer,' by Brenda Byers. Again, Tommy was smoking it. We slowed down a bit and did our version of 'Blue Ridge Mountain Boy.' By now the crowd had edged up to the stage and were looking on and cheering after some of Tommy's riffs and whoopin' and hollerin' when we finished a song. Well, the rest of the band picked it up and pretty soon my boys were playing like the Buck Owens band."

Wes nodded. "I can just see it in my mind's eye."

Josie took a deep breath. "After we had played a few tunes, he leaned over and asked me if I knew 'Love is no excuse.' Well, I did. Tommy took the Jim Reeves part, and I sang Dottie West. Well, before we finished, I guess someone put the word out, because the place started filling up like it was first set on a Friday night. That bar started jumpin'. When we finished that song, the place came apart. So, we did a few more standards, then Tommy asked if he could do a special. We were on a roll and we all said sure, so he called out 'Ghost Riders in the Sky.' Look out Roy Clark. Tommy Franklin blew the walls out with his version. When he finished, the place went nuts, I mean absolutely nuts. And at the end of the set, the owner came over and offered us a six-week contract, with the stipulation that Tommy join our band." Josie smiled. "That's when I met Tommy, the negotiator. He stepped right in before I could say yes and whispered in my ear, 'What is he paying you?' Two hundred a night, I whispered back. Tommy grinned. 'Watch this,' he says. Before I knew it, he had us booked for four hundred a night and a cut of the bar over a thousand dollars. And he got the owner to go for an extension if we did good. Well, the long and short of it is we ended up playing there six months. By the end of the booking, we were pulling down a thousand a night plus a hefty cut of the bar. And we were now The Red Hot Country Mamas featuring Tommy Franklin."

Josie looked over at Wes and saw the question in his eyes. "Yes, Wes, I went home with Tommy that night. He was staying in a crummy motel outside of town and after we hung out a few days, I had him bring his stuff and come stay with me at my place. We were hot and heavy and didn't cool off for a while. He was there for over a year."

She glanced over and saw a look on Wes's face. It cut her like a knife. She turned away.

"I know, Wes, I know. I was a fool. But I was lonely, and he seemed to be just what I needed. I thought... I thought I loved him. Maybe I did, but he didn't love me. He just used me. Like everyone does." Josie put her head down and felt something in her face she hadn't felt for a long time—the hot flush of shame. She wished she could just disappear. Then she felt something else—burning anger. It made her bold. She stood up and pointed a quivering finger at Wes.

"I see how you're lookin' at me. Don't judge me, Wes. There was a time in my life I was a good girl. I knew what right and wrong was. Then that pervert Ted got a hold of me. When you found out about Ted, you tossed me aside like a piece of trash. Oh, maybe not physically, right off, but in your heart, you did. You let me know I was spoiled goods, so I figured that's what I was. A piece of trash, garbage. So, I only acted like what you let me know I was."

Wes looked away. "I'm not judging you, Josie. I'm judging me. You are absolutely right. What I did to you was unconscionable. I know I hurt you real bad, and you'll carry the scars all your life, unless you can find healing somehow."

Josie laughed out loud. "Yeah right! And just how am I supposed to find this healing?"

"I think it might start if you could forgive me."

"Man, you throw that word around pretty easy, Wes. Just how am I supposed to forgive you? You walked out on your family. You had a wife who would have loved you forever. Don't you remember the song? That stupid song."

"I remember."

"Well, it wasn't just a song. When you got me to write the lyrics, it wasn't just some kind of literary exercise. It was real. It came out of my heart. I just wanted you to keep on loving me, to tell me you loved me. To never stop loving me. That's all I wanted. I thought you were in my life to save me. I pinned all my hopes on you..." Josie felt a sob start in her throat. "All my hopes..." She flung herself down on the couch. "What a fool I was." She buried her face in her hands.

Wes got up and came over to her. He knelt down in front of her, took her hands in his. She fought him, tried to keep him from holding her prisoner, tried to wrench her hands free. He was too strong.

His hands are so big, so warm.

He said nothing, just stayed like that in front of her... silent.

Finally, she looked up at him. Startled, she could see that tears were streaming down his face. He kissed each one of her hands slowly. She could feel the wetness of his tears. And then she felt something stir in her heart. Like being in a cool mountain stream, pure clean. The feeling scared her, almost overwhelmed her. He kissed her hands again. Then his voice broke the quiet. Deep, full of strength, full of... something... she didn't know...

"I know I betrayed you, I know I ruined everything, but, Josie, honey... I never stopped loving you. I swear. I swear."

Josie pulled his hands. Not to get away this time... but to bring him to her. He came up beside her. And then his arms were around her and he was kissing her face. Not her lips at first, but her cheeks, her eyes, her ears and then... finally... her lips. Gentle, not hard like he wanted something from her, but easy, deep, just his lips on hers, no forcing, but leading, his hands holding her face, and she wanted to just climb into him, this Wes, this man that she knew but didn't know.

It was around dusk. After the blow-up, they sat for a long time in each other's arms. Outside, the westering sun was casting long shadows from the bare tree limbs. They had not moved for a long time, just soaking, being. She surprised herself. The kisses had not been about lust. They were something so far beyond sex she was glad he had not gone any further. Finally, she spoke.

"What was that, Wes? I've never felt anything like that. It wasn't passion, it was so deep and comforting, so kind."

"It's love, Josie, what love is supposed to be. I just want you to see how much I love you. I don't want anything from you. I just want to give you something without taking anything in return. It took me a long time to figure out the difference." He reached into the pocket of his shirt and took out a folded piece of paper. He unfolded it and read the words. "Love is patient and kind;

love does not envy or boast; it is not arrogant or rude. It does not insist on its own way; it is not irritable or resentful; it does not rejoice at wrongdoing, but rejoices with the truth. Love bears all things, believes all things, hopes all things, endures all things."

Josie looked at him. This Wes. This different Wes. "That's beautiful. But nobody can love like that... can they?"

Wes shook his head. "I take this out and read it to myself at least once a day. It reminds me how far away from truth I can get. It reminds me that the things I want to do, I don't do and the things I don't want to do, I do. But it also shows me I can have something to aspire to, something that's beyond the demands of my body or my mind. Something that's just true. And it helps me to be true. And that's what I want my life to be... true, straight, honest."

She reached her hand up and touched his face, softly, lingering. He took her hand and kissed it again.

"Wes, oh, Wes. Can I trust you? If I surrender, will you hold my heart in gentle hands? I'm frightened, Wes. I'm frightened because I'm going to die, and I don't know what's beyond, what's out there. And maybe, maybe if someone could just help me see what's true and straight and honest, what's real... maybe I could come to grips with my life. Oh, Wes, I don't want to finish badly. Can you help me, Wes? Is that why you're here?"

He nodded and stroked her hair. "That's all I want to do, Josie, to help you. To be here for you, to love you, to show you real love."

"Oh Wes, what is that? I have never known genuine love. All the places, all the men, all the lovers..."

"I haven't got it all figured out, but I guess I think that love, real love, is about sacrifice and unconditional care. The Greeks had a word for it... Agape. The way they saw it, the truest love transcended feelings and was about actions and commitment. You see, back then, when we were together, I didn't know that the reason a man stays married is not because he feels good about the person he's married to, but because he gave his word. I didn't know that I couldn't be a man if I couldn't keep my promise... my promise to you. It's taken me a long time, and some long trails to bring me to that place. So that's what brought me here. I promised you a long time ago that I would love you forever and always take care of you, and now I want to keep that promise. No matter what happens, I want you to live inside my promise, until the day..." He struggled to go on, but couldn't.

Josie suddenly saw that the great dividing moment of her life was now before her. She had two choices. She could believe this man and give herself over into his care and love, or she could reject him and go on alone, into the darkness. And a great fear rose in her, a fear of being by herself when she died. A fear of not having someone to love her just for who she was, not for what they could get. Suddenly she was in his arms again, holding him desperately with all her strength, weeping.

"Yes, Wes, Yes."

"What, honey?"

"I'll marry you, I'll marry you, Wes."

Their faces pressed together and she could feel his smile. "When, Josie?"

"Tomorrow, as soon as the sun rises."

Chapter Eighteen

CARING

Wes smiled and kissed Josie on the forehead. "Not so fast, girlie. Oregon has a three-day waiting period. We can go down and apply tomorrow morning, but we can't get married until Thursday."

Josie looked at him. "You're not from Oregon. How did you know that?"

Wes shrugged. "I checked already."

"Pretty sure of yourself, cowboy."

"Well, let's just say I was hoping you would say yes, so I went out and acted like you already did. I read somewhere 'hope that is seen is not hope.'"

Josie looked at Wes. "You're a funny guy, Wes. It's like I know you, but I don't know you."

"The years change us, Josie. At least we can hope they do. Oh, and another thing we will need is a witness."

"A witness?"

"Yes, someone to witness that we really got married."

"Who can we get?"

"How about the lady at the end of the driveway?"

"Amanda?" Josie frowned. "Oh, sheesh. I don't know. I was

cold as a Texas blizzard to her. I basically told her to take a hike and don't come back."

Wes shook his head. "Well, we could walk down together and ask her."

"I'm embarrassed."

"Come on, honey. I'll be with you."

So, the next morning, they walked down to Amanda's house. Wes went up and knocked, and Josie stood awkwardly at his side. Amanda opened the door and, to Josie's relief, smiled and stepped out to hug her. It was genuine and Josie felt a little like a horse's hind end.

"Josie. Good to see you. Gosh, it's been…"

"Eight weeks and three days."

Amanda smiled. "Come on in. Ben's up and doing pretty good."

They stepped inside. A voice came from the front room. "Amanda?"

Amanda looked toward the living room. "In a minute, Ben." She smiled at Wes. "Who's this?"

Josie looked up at Wes. He saved her by reaching out his hand and smiling his famous smile. "I'm Wesley James Branson. Josie and I were married a long time ago. I heard about… well, her trouble, and I came to help. To get right to the point, we have a favor to ask you."

"Favor?"

Josie felt herself blushing.

Really awkward.

"We're getting married… again… and we need someone to stand up with us. Would you, please?"

Amanda looked from Josie to Wes, and then back to Josie. Then she smiled. "Of course, I will, Wesley." She stepped forward and pulled Josie into a hug. Josie's arms went around her and she whispered in Amanda's ear.

"I was a complete jerk. I mean, the way I ran you off. You were just trying to help, and I wasn't in a very trusting place. I don't know why you'd even want to look at me, but I'm very grateful for your help."

Amanda put her hands on Josie's shoulders and held her away for a minute. She looked at Wes. "Wesley...,"

He grinned. "Just Wes is fine."

"Okay, Wes. There's coffee on the stove and cups in the rack. I need to talk to this lady for a minute." As Wes headed for the kitchen, she pulled Josie into a side room. "You look different. Something in your eyes. Peace. It wasn't there when I met you."

Josie sank down on the bed. "When Wes showed up, he was the last person in the world I wanted to see. I thought I hated him more than anybody. Well... almost. But he's been here for two months and he's taken all the crap I could throw at him. He's never complained, totally been here for me. He's just... loved me. And finally, I saw that..."

"You could trust him?"

"I saw I had come to a big fork in my trail. I could either go on alone, hating myself, hating everyone else, and end up badly, dying alone in my bed in a dark room. Or..."

"Or?"

Josie nodded. "Or... I could put myself into this man's hands and have someone to be with me to the end, maybe carry me the last few yards."

"And Wes will do that?"

"He says he will. And I have had to do something I have never done before."

Amanda put her hand on Josie's shoulder. "Have faith in someone? Trust them?"

Josie nodded again. "When we were married, we were just kids. He knew nothing, and neither did I, especially about how to make a marriage work. I didn't have a real dad..." Josie shuddered at the memory... "and my mom was a drunk. So, nobody ever helped me, told me, guided me. I was alone at sea on a piece of bark, and when the storm came, I got swept away."

"And now Wes is here."

"Yes, Wes is here. And you know something, Amanda? I haven't got the faintest idea how that happened. All I know is that Wes has changed. He's the same, but he's different. He's grown up and all man."

Amanda smiled. "The tough trails will do that to a boy. My Ted was a ne'er-do-well when I met him. But he got a crazy hair when we met and decided, I guess, that he wanted me bad and he'd do anything to get me. And from then on..."

"Yeah, it's like that with Wes now. He went away one day, and he went through hellfire and it seems to have burned all the bark off him. I guess I don't know how that works."

Amanda looked out the window, then back. "I have my own idea about that, but I won't push it."

Josie felt something flick her inside, where the darkness was. She hesitated and then... "If it is God, Amanda, you can share it. I know I haven't always seen eye-to-eye with Christians, but you'd have to know my story."

"Somebody who said they were a Christian hurt you real bad."

Josie looked up in surprise and the words just came out. "Yeah, my stepdad."

"Josie, sweetie, a minute ago you said you had come to a fork in the road. Part of that fork is growing to understand that God is not a man, and the things that men do in His name rarely have anything to do with what He really wants for us. If you can keep Him separate from the skunks that stink up the church, you'll see Him at work all around you and in your life. And that's all I'm gonna say because I'm like a brush fire when I get going." She grinned at Josie's grateful smile.

"Love that you can smile, honey. Now let's get that man of yours and get downtown. We got some things to take care of."

THE FIRST STOP was the County Clerk's office. Amanda introduced them to the gray-haired lady behind the desk in the front. "Willie, this is Wes and Josie. They've come for a marriage license."

"Well, bless your hearts." Willie waved at some chairs. "Sit, sit, and we'll get you all set up. Got any ID?"

Wes grinned and then drawled. "'Bout what?"

Willie looked at Wes and then burst into laughter. "Oh, I like him. Texican?"

Wes nodded. "Yes, ma'am. Josie too. Laredo."

"Corpus Christie, myself. Just a whoop and a holler away."

"Yep, did a little rodeo over there."

"Any good?"

Wes shrugged. "I thought I was until I climbed aboard a man-killer bull named Bone-breaker, over in California. When I woke up I was a Marine."

They all laughed. Willie started over. "Okay, let's see some personal identification."

Wes and Josie pulled out their driver's licenses. Wes looked at his Texas license. "Do I have to be a resident?"

Willie smiled and took the licenses and looked them over. "Nope, no residency requirement, and I see by these that you're both over eighteen, so we don't have to worry about that." She handed over a piece of paper. "Fill this out, please, and I will need sixty bucks. Check or cash works best."

Willy waited for a minute while Wes pulled his wallet out. "You're not cousins, are you?"

Josie smiled. "I sure hope not."

"That's good because you can't marry your cousin in Burns, Oregon. I also got to ask about divorce. Ever been?"

Josie giggled and Wes blushed. "Yeah, she divorced me thirty years ago. And rightly so."

Willie laughed. "Second-timers, huh? Well, sometimes you got to go around the quad a few times to figure it out. I get several 'deucers' a year in here."

Wes finished his part of the form and signed it. Josie took it and filled in her information, but when she got to the signature line, something in her balked. She sat there staring at the form. Then she felt a hand on her shoulder. "Cold feet?"

She turned and looked into Wes's eyes. She just looked until she saw what she wanted. There was no deceit there. "No, Wes, no cold feet." She signed her name and handed it to Willie.

"Y'all got three days to wait and this papers good for only sixty days. So get'er done. And congratulations. Where you gonna get married?"

Josie and Wes looked at each other.

"In a church? Justice of the Peace? City hall? Lots of places."

Wes shrugged. "We haven't really talked about it."

"Well, you got three days to decide. Here." Willie slid a piece of paper across the desk. "Maybe this will help. This is a list of everyone who does weddings in Burns—addresses and phone numbers."

Josie took the paper. "Thank you, Willie."

They went out to Wes's truck and headed back to the ranchette. After they dropped Amanda off, they went into the house and Josie made some coffee. When they sat, Wes asked a question.

"What was the end of the Tommy Franklin story?"

"What do you mean?"

"You said that I was involved somehow."

"Oh, right. Well, he stole our song."

"What?"

"Yeah. I knew nothing about copyrights or protecting my tunes. When we were together, I showed him Hummingbirds. He worked up an arrangement, featuring his guitar, of course, and we played it a lot. It was our most requested song. What I didn't know was that he filed the copyright in his name. Oh, he put our names on it and gave us a tiny piece, but the copyright was in his name. And he changed the Josie and Wes line to Tommy and Bess or something stupid. I didn't know it until the end of our relationship."

"What did he do with it?" Wes had a strange look on his face, one that kind of scared Josie.

"Well, he hooked up with a manager and went off to Nashville. From what I heard, he was trying to peddle the song. He was also trying to get a record deal for himself, but what he didn't know is that the folks who make it in Nashville stay pretty straight most of the time."

"And he didn't?"

"No, he was a drunk and a pothead. Totally unreliable. After he blew off a few sessions, the word was out on the street and he couldn't get work. That's why he ended up in Burns."

"He's here?"

"Last I heard, he got a steady gig with his band at the Silver Mine. At least he was there a week ago. Saw it in the paper."

Wes stood up. "You know, Josie, I just thought of something I have to take care of. You look over that list and when I get back, we'll make the call."

She didn't like the look on his face.

"Where are you going, Wes?"

"Oh, just going to go get something back that I lost. I won't be long."

And then he was out the door.

Chapter Nineteen

LOST AND FOUND

Wes was gone for several hours. When he returned Josie heard him come in the back door to the kitchen and stop there for a minute. She heard some bags rustling and then he came in and he was smiling. Josie confronted him. "You look like the cat who ate the canary. What's going on? Where did you go?"

Wes smiled his half-smile, but Josie didn't buy it. "You've done something. What did you do?"

Wes handed Josie a folded piece of paper. She opened it. It was a legal document signed by Tommy Franklin, and someone that appeared to be a notary public. Josie read it.

I, Tommy Franklin, do hereby relinquish all claims to the song "When the Hummingbirds Danced in a Honeysuckle Sky" and assign any and all rights that I may have had or imagined I had to Josie Winters of Burns, Oregon (domiciled at 71885 Highway 20, Burns, OR, 97720), the actual writer of this song. Any copyright claims to "When the Hummingbirds Danced in a Honeysuckle Sky" I hereby relinquish and I also quit any other claims or rights to this song.

Signed Tommy Franklin

Witnessed by Leroy Parkins, Notary Public

There was a seal and some official language below the signatures. Josie stared at it. "How in the world did you get him to sign this?"

Wes reached inside his jacket and pulled out a packet in a brown mailer. He handed it to Josie. It was addressed to Margaret Branson in Laredo, Texas. The postmark read 1967 and it had foreign looking stamps, and then she saw it had never been opened. "Do you know what's in there, Josie?"

She shook her head. "I have no idea." They both chuckled, remembering Wes's joke at the County Clerk's office.

"Do you remember the little book I used to write lyric ideas in?"

"Yes. You had it that first night we saw the hummingbirds. You wrote down a few thoughts I had."

"Right. And then when we wrote the song I wrote it all down in the book."

"What does that have to do with Tommy Franklin?"

"Give me a minute." He went out to the kitchen and came back with a couple of paper plates with some Colonel Sanders on it. "Thought you might be hungry."

He sat and started eating.

"Wesley James Branson, you tell me what you did. I mean it."

"Okay, okay don't get your knickers in a knot." He took another bite and then grinned at the concerned look on her face. "No, I did not beat Tommy Franklin into a flat piece of road kill. I had a very genial conversation with him. I went down to the Silver Mine and he was there, practicing with the band. When I told him who I was, his eyes got real big and he took me back in the dressing room. I guess he knew I had something to say that the band guys shouldn't be in on. Then I showed him this package."

"How did that get him to sign this letter."

Wes shrugged. "When I was in Nam I met a guy, another guitar player, and we kinda fooled around with writing some songs when we were off-duty. I showed him *Hummingbirds*. He asked me if I had it copyrighted. I didn't know anything about it so he gave me some tips. Then he said that the best thing to do before I got back to where I could take care of it, was to send the song in a package to my mom and tell her not to open it. So, I sent my little book, dated February 1967."

Josie was fascinated. "She never opened it?"

"Nope. I sent it with a letter telling her I needed it to stay sealed. You see, that postmark on an unopened letter is just as valid as a copyright and proves that I wrote the song before that date. When my mom died, I found this in her stuff. I never opened it either. And then I got so busy, I didn't get around to filing a copyright. I've carried it around with me ever since. Don't know why, but now I know. A little wisdom from above, maybe."

That's an odd thing to say...

"Well, I asked Tommy the same question I asked you—did he know what was in here? 'Course he didn't. When I told him, I added a few more details, like copyright theft or lying on a government form is a crime and I would be happy to send his name to the proper authorities. I told him that I knew that the copyright he filed was dated way after my package's date and I would be happy to point that out in a court of law—which meant that he stole the song and he knew it. Well, he got kinda limp in the knees and asked me what I wanted. So, I rustled him into the truck and took him down to the County Clerk. Willie had a notary public in the office and we whipped up a little quit claim deed, he signed it, and the song is yours. Forever."

"And you didn't whup him or threaten him?"

"Nope, I was nice as could be, a real gentleman."

Wes laughed and the sound was like deep bells on a quiet morning.

He protected me. He went after what I lost and he found it.

Then Josie realized something. The darkness was gone from her heart.

Me. I'm what was lost and Wes found me. He found me and now I'm not lost anymore.

She looked at Wes and all she felt was love, and then, admiration. He was her man. He did love her. And peace like a river came flowing through her soul... followed by the "It".

Wes got her up and got her into bed. The pain was so intense she almost screamed. He got her medicine and she got it down with some water. The pain subsided after a while. Wes sat by her bed the whole time until she fell asleep. He looked at her face. Perspiration had matted her hair and her skin was pale. He stroked her sleeping face softly. Wes Branson looked down at the woman he loved and then bowed his head and prayed. He prayed for Josie, he prayed for the future, he wept. And when he finished he reminded God that whatever He had for them, Wesley James Branson would do what he could to make the days to come good days for Josie.

Josie was lights out most of the next day, but by evening she had come around and was back to normal, if there was a 'normal' with the "It" lurking in the background. She came out of her room all gussied up. Wes was sitting on the couch and his eyes lit up when he saw her.

"Still the prettiest gal in town."

She smiled. "Yeah, I clean up pretty good." She handed him the list of folks that would marry them. She had circled one of the names—Reverend Johnny Sparks. Wes looked up in surprise. "But this guy is a Christian."

"Yeah, well, I might be backing off on my stand... just a little."

Wes motioned for her to sit down. "What's this about, Josie?"

She took a deep breath. "Couple of things. One, Amanda said

something to me the other day that made a whole lot of sense. She said that what men do in God's name and what God does on his own are two completely different things. She said if I could learn to separate the two, I might see God at work all around me."

Wes nodded.

"You know, Wes, I used to believe in God, before Ted got at me. I had a little Bible my Grandma gave me and I read it all the time. I remember it was white and it had my name in gold print on the bottom—Josie Marie Winters. I loved it. I used to keep it under my pillow at night because I thought it had magical powers. I wanted to be a good girl but I didn't know how to go about it. Then my dad died and my mom married Ted and then the bad stuff started. I blamed God, I guess. I mean, how could a God who was supposed to love the whole world let my dad die and then let my mom marry a monster like Ted?"

"Those are good questions. We can talk about it, but first tell me the other thing."

Josie took another breath. "The other thing... okay. The other night, when I was in such bad shape, I think you thought the morphine knocked me out. But it didn't."

She saw that he blushed. "Oh...," he said.

"Yeah, I was awake. I heard you pray for me." She moved over into his arms. She got as close to him as she could. "Oh, Wes. It was so beautiful. You prayed over me, you cried over me, you asked God to help me and be with me. And then you promised God you would see me through this, no matter what happened. I... I've never had anybody love me that way. Oh, Wes, oh, Wes. We missed so many good things."

Josie began to weep on his shoulder, soft sobs that came up from the depth of her soul. Somehow it was so safe, the strength of his arms, the man-smell of him, his hands caressing her hair softly. It was like a pure, rushing, mountain stream that came into her heart and began to wash away the debris and the stains, and the wrack and ruin of her life. "I love you, Wes. I've always loved you. I was so lost and then you came back for me."

She swallowed hard and looked up at his face. "Wes... I forgive you. I don't have any more anger. All I feel is this frightful, terrifying love for you that's almost crushing my heart."

He kissed her cheek gently. "You're the only girl I ever loved, Josie. I never stopped, even through all those years. I've said it before and I'll say it once more. I'm so sorry for what I did. I'll have the regret from it for the rest of my life. But I'm here to say that the rest of our time together, whatever God gives us, I will do my very best to make it a blessing for you. All my love, my strength, my life, will be focused on you. I promise." He pulled back and looked into her eyes. She could see that he had been crying, too. "Thank you for forgiving me, Josie. It's the best wedding present I could ever ask for."

He reached for a tissue in a box on the table and gently wiped her eyes... then his. "Now let's call the Reverend Johnny Sparks and see about getting hitched."

She hugged him again. "I can't wait, Wesley James Branson, I can't wait."

THE HUMMINGBIRDS SONG...

My dad told me later when he got the song back for Josie, it was like all his life finally made sense. He said it was like he had come to the great resolution of all that he was meant to do and be in this life. What he didn't tell me about was his faith. Not then at least. A faith he found on the killing fields of Vietnam, in the eyes of a dying friend. A faith that took root in his heart and carried him down some lonesome trails until it brought him to Burns, Oregon and the place where God had always wanted him to be—walking beside Josie Winters, soon to be Mrs. Wesley James Branson.

Margi

Chapter Twenty

WEDDING DAY

It was April 6, 2005, 8:00 in the morning. Josie Winters stood in front of the mirror, putting the final touches on her wedding dress. It was pale pink, simple and sleeveless with a not immodest plunging neckline. She had a pale pink hand-knit silk and merino bridal shawl that draped beautifully around her shoulders. She looked at herself in the mirror.

One more journey, Josie, only this time, Wes will be with you.

There was a knock on the door.

"It's Amanda, honey."

Josie went to the door and opened it a crack to make sure Wes wasn't there.

Amanda followed her glance. "He's gone to town, Josie. He wanted to make sure the church was set to go, and he knew you wanted to surprise him with your dress, so I kicked him out of here." She stepped into the room. "He... oh, Josie, honey... you look lovely."

Josie blushed. She so wanted to be beautiful for Wes. Her red hair picked up some lights from the morning sun and flamed against the pink shawl. Josie ran her hand over the smooth material. "Thank you for this shawl, Amanda. It is so perfect. I..." Josie reached over and took Amanda's hand. "I need to say something to you. You have showed me what friendship can be. I was so mean to you, very mean, and yet you never changed, and now you're standing up with me. It means everything to me."

Amanda took Josie in her arms. "I was too pushy with you and you had a right to send me packing. But I knew we were meant to be friends, so I just looked at my own attitudes and approaches and made a few changes. Thank you for helping me do that."

JOSIE WINTERS WAS in a strange and different land. It was as though she had come to a sign beside a road through a strange and dark wilderness; a sign that said, 'Beyond this place... there be dragons.' But she went on anyway, though she did not know the way. And then she found the dragons, the deepest fears of her darkest dreams, weren't really dragons after all. And instead of the door into a dragon's lair where only despair lurked and hurt was the emotion du jour, she had somehow come through the door of love. She could not remember ever feeling this way in her whole life.

As Amanda drove her to the church, Josie felt the years fall away, and she was Josie Winters again, young, and full of life and... well, not exactly full of life. Her body was betraying her. As she looked out the window, she felt a tiny twinge of pain deep inside, a starting. She gasped, but by sheer willpower she fought it back.

No! You will not win today. This is my day, mine and Wes's, and you have no part in it. You may win another day, but not this day.

And it was as though her thoughts took wings and became a prayer, and someone was listening, because she felt the pain back away, like a lion does obeisance to the man with the chair and the whip, snarling yet cowed. And for the first time in a long time, she recognized the connection between her and something much bigger, greater, beyond her senses or sensibilities. A... person? A... power? She did not know what it was, but she felt it.

She had risen that morning early, as the sun rose quietly in the East, and as she stood at the open window, she smelled lilacs. The fragrance of spring, of new life, of a world coming awake after the deep sleep of winter's death. In that stillness, she bowed her head and asked... the power... the person... for a perfect day, and somehow, when she lifted her head, she knew her wish would be granted.

Amanda heard her gasp and looked over. "You okay, honey?"

Josie nodded, then looked down at her bouquet, white roses with a pink blush, and whispered. "Why do you love me?"

And it was a question for Wes, and for Amanda, and for whoever or whatever was revealing themself to her in that moment. And the answer came, almost like a voice in her heart.

I just do.

WHEN THEY GOT to the church, Amanda took Josie around to the pastor's office. The sign on the door said Reverend Johnny Sparks, Pastor. Amanda led the way in and Josie followed, feeling shy... about as local as a fish in a tree. The pastor was behind the desk but got up immediately.

"Amanda Sacks, haven't seen you since Sunday." He grinned, then turned to Josie. "My, my my! This must be Josie. Wes is a lucky man."

Josie felt the blush flood her face.

I feel like I'm thirteen years old.

Pastor Sparks came around the desk and reached out a hand. Josie handed the bouquet to Amanda and then shook his hand. He looked at his watch. "Wes went out to get something about an hour ago. He should be back any minute. Sit down." He pointed to a chair. Josie carefully arranged her dress and sat.

"So, this is the second time around?"

Josie nodded. "It's a long story, Pastor. But I feel as though I am finally exactly where I'm supposed to be. And, the funny thing is, I had that feeling the day I drove into Burns back in August, before I knew I was sick, before I met Amanda, before Wes came to help. I didn't know any of this would happen. I just feel like someone, maybe God, has given me a chance to set some things right in my life. I'm not sure how that all works because I haven't seen eye-to-eye with Him for a long, long time."

"Well, I met Wes yesterday and I can tell you, I liked him right off. He's got his head screwed on straight and he loves you like life itself."

Josie hesitated and then asked. "You know, Pastor, we haven't been to counseling or anything. Will we be okay?"

Pastor Johnny smiled. "Well, Josie, I had a long talk with Wes yesterday and from what he tells me, you two have been working through a lot of your issues already. Sometimes a pastor just gets a sense of things, a small look at what God is doing in people's lives. To tell you the truth, I feel that the good Lord is right in the middle of this marriage. I have no doubt whatever that you two were made for each other—that you were made for each other a long time ago, but you just made some choices that took you down different roads. And now the circle is closed, and here you are. So, I'm blessed to be the one who gets to do the honors. I really am."

Josie felt tears starting, but Amanda stepped in and quickly and expertly dabbed them away, saving her makeup. Just then, there was a knock at the door. Pastor Johnny went and opened it a crack. Josie heard Wes's voice and then Johnny nodded his head, reached out and took something from Wes. He closed the door and turned to Josie. "Wes went out and got this for you. He thought you might like to carry it."

Johnny handed Josie a small wrapped box. She sat back down and took off the wrapping. Underneath was a small plain white box. Josie opened the box. Inside was a beautiful, leather-covered white Bible with a golden cross embossed on the cover. Down at the bottom in gold letters was a name—Josie Marie Branson. She stared at it and then put her hands to her face. "Oh, Wes. Oh, Wes."

She looked up at Johnny and Amanda. Amanda had tears on her cheeks. Johnny pretended that something was making his eye itch.

Johnny took a breath and smiled. "I think it's time we got you folks married. Are you ready, Josie?"

Josie nodded. "Yes, yes I am, Pastor."

"Okay, I figure Amanda can walk you down the aisle."

"Would you, Amanda?"

"Right there, honey. It's an honor."

"So, when you hear the music..."

"Music?"

"Oh, I guess I forgot to tell you. My wife is the church pianist, and she said every wedding needs music so she's rarin' to go. See you in a minute."

Josie Winters suddenly felt an incredible excitement fill her body. It was such an intense rush that she gasped out loud. Amanda looked at her. "You okay, honey?"

Josie smiled. "Yes, Amanda. I am more okay than I have ever been in my whole life. I'm going to marry Wes. I can't believe it. I'm going to marry Wes."

From outside, Josie heard piano music. But it wasn't the wedding march, it was the old Floyd Cramer song, 'Forever in Love.' The pastor's wife was playing it slow and country, beautifully, like Floyd would, and a thrill went down Josie's spine. Amanda took her elbow and guided her through the door, down a short hallway, and into the sanctuary of the little church. Josie looked up. Wesley James Branson stood by the pastor at the end of the aisle. He had on a dark suit, a white shirt, a beautiful white Stetson hat, and a red string tie. His broad shoulders filled the suit jacket and his slim rider's hips made him look the man he was. He saw Josie and a look of wonder crossed his face. No one had ever looked at her like that, and for the first time in her life, she felt like a woman, a woman whose man loved her and wanted her just for her. It was the most real and wonderful feeling she had ever felt.

She walked with the bouquet held on top of her Bible. It seemed like she would never get there. And then Amanda was taking her bouquet and Bible and handing her off to Wes. Wes took both her hands in his. She felt the strength of his hands.

Johnny looked at Wes and asked, "Do you have the rings?"

Josie's heart jumped.

The rings? Oh, I don't have...

Wes smiled and put his finger to his lips.

"Sure do, Pastor."

He reached into his pocket and pulled out a little jeweler's box. He opened it. Inside were two plain gold bands, a man's and a woman's. He handed them to Johnny.

"But where...?"

Wes smiled again. "It was my mother's ring. I got a gold one to match for me."

Wes! Oh, Wes. You've known for weeks!

Josie looked at Wes as the pastor spoke. She really didn't hear anything because she was lost in Wes—his eyes, his face, the warmth of his hands. And then she saw the pastor hand Wes the small ring.

"Do you, Wesley, take this woman to be your wife?

"I do."

"Wes, do you have something you want to say to Josie?"

Wes slipped the ring onto Josie's finger. It fit perfectly. He took her hands in his and looked straight into her soul.

"With this ring, Josie Marie, I pledge my love to you today and for the rest of our lives. I will be the laughter in your tears and the calm in your storms. I vow to support you through the darkest times, to bring you comfort when you are in pain, and to celebrate every victory, no matter how small. With every step we take, I promise to cherish you, to protect you, and to be your love, your friend, and your partner for all our days. I have loved you since the moment I met you and I will love you forever."

Pastor Johnny smiled and handed Josie the other ring.

"Do you, Josie, take this man to be your husband?"

"I do."

She took Wes's hand in her hands. She slipped the ring onto his finger and then covered his hand with both of hers. She thought about the words that had been brimming in her heart, that she had been rehearsing to herself for three days.

"Wesley James Branson, you are the only man I have ever loved. In this life... in this life and beyond, I choose you. I vow to love you with every breath I take and every beat of my heart. For the time we have together, I promise to love you with every fiber of my being. Through all the highs and lows to come, I will never give up on us. I will trust you and believe in you, and hold on to our love until my last breath. I promise."

Pastor Johnny took their hands and put them together. "On hearing your vows and promises, by the authority vested in me by the State of Oregon, I pronounce you husband and wife. Mr. and Mrs. Wesley James Branson."

JOSIE AND WES... AGAIN

Josie and Wes, Wes and Josie. Two tumbleweeds that drifted along by themselves for years and yet somehow ended up lodged against the same barbed-wire fence in Burns, Oregon, in the fourth year of the Twenty-first century. Josie and Wes, my mother and father. I was not there when they got married again, but I know from my mother's letters to me and the things my dad has shared that it was a perfect day. Perfect except for knowing their time together would be short. But despite that, what I know is that they both purposed in their hearts to make their remaining time together a time of love, a time of joy, and a time of wonder. There's just a little more to the story, but the ending is, like their wedding day, perfect in every way.

Margi

Chapter Twenty-One

BEYOND THIS PLACE

When they came out of the church, the sun was shining and spring had burst upon Bend, Oregon. The smell of lilacs was in the air, and a cool breeze rustled the new growth that was springing forth on every tree. Josie's hand was in Wes's and she looked up at him. There seemed to be a softness in his face that she had never seen before.

I've changed... but he's changed too.

He looked down at her and smiled, the half-smile that made him so handsome. "Well, Mrs. Branson, Amanda, has something planned for us down at the Lemon Tree..."

Josie lifted her arms, and Wes took her in. She whispered in his ear.

"Mrs. Branson. Wes, I'm Mrs. Branson again. The only thing I ever wanted to be. Thank you, thank you."

They stood that way for a long time, with the sun smiling down on them. Finally, Wes spoke. "We are going to have a little brunch and then we are going on a trip. Did you pack your things?"

"Yes, but they're back at the house."

Wes shook his head. "No, they're in my truck."

"But I have to change."

"No problem. Mrs. Sparks said you can change at the parsonage. It's right next door. Then we'll take off. We have a six-hour drive."

A honeymoon. We're going on a honeymoon!

"Where are we going, Wes? Tell me?"

He put his finger to her lips. "Someplace exquisite, just like you. That's all I'm saying."

"Have you been there?"

"No, but I heard about it, so I checked it out, and I quizzed Amanda, and it seems to be a wonderful place. Special for my special girl."

Mrs. Sparks and Amanda came out. Mrs. Sparks took Josie's hand. "Do you have your things?"

"Yes, Wes brought them. Thank you, Mrs. Sparks."

"Please, call me Elaine. Okay, Amanda has some business at the restaurant. I'll help you get ready and we'll go down to the reception."

"Reception?"

"Can't have a wedding without a reception."

Josie turned to Amanda. "Did you plan this?"

Amanda grinned. "Who else? Oh, it's just a little brunch to celebrate. You need your strength for your honeymoon trip."

"Do you know where we are going?"

Amanda just smiled. "Wes needed some input, didn't he? I mean, having never been to Oregon. All I can say is, you will love it."

Josie changed at the parsonage. Elaine took the wedding dress, slipped a plastic bag over it, and told Josie she would take care of it until they returned. Then they drove to the Lemon Tree Restaurant where they had a delicious lunch specially prepared by the chef. Josie finished and was gathering her things when the servers came in with a beautiful cake. She looked over at Amanda.

"Did you make this?"

Amanda smiled. "Right in my kitchen. Gotta have a cake."

All the staff gathered around and applauded while Josie and Wes cut the cake and then they all had a piece. Josie looked at all the smiling faces. Wes stood by her, not saying much, but speaking to her with a look or a touch of the hand.

I belong. I belong to someone who really loves me.

Wes leaned over and whispered. "You ready to go? We have a fairly long drive."

I'll go anywhere with you. I don't care how long it takes.

She nodded and took his hand.

Wes made a little speech, thanking the pastor and his wife, and the staff at the restaurant, and especially their friend, Amanda. Then he led Josie out to the truck. There was a 'Just Married' sign in the back window and some cans tied on the bumper. Josie smiled and waved out of the window as some people threw rice.

Like Cinderella going home from the ball with the prince. My prince.

THEY DROVE through some desert country until they got to the town of Ontario, and then they turned north and headed up Highway 84. They passed through rugged, dry country until they came down a long hill to a place called Farewell Bend.

Wes pointed to the river on their right. "That's the Snake. Right here it takes a hard-right turn and dumps into Hell's Canyon. The Oregon Trail came right through here and the wagon trains ended up on the far side of the river. They crossed here. Pretty rugged, lots of folks drowned or were swept away into the canyon. The river in there was as wild as the Colorado in the Grand Canyon until they put a couple of dams in."

They kept going and soon came down a long hill into Baker

City, Oregon. They stopped for gas and had a light snack at the restaurant behind the station. Then north again until they got to LaGrande, where they turned off the freeway. Soon they were heading up into pine tree country, following a road along a river. They came to a little town called Elgin and headed east. There was a mill in town and the wigwam burner was pumping out pine smoke. It smelled wonderful.

Josie gazed in wonder at the tree-covered hills. A medium-sized mountain range hung on the horizon to the north as they drove up and over a long ridge. They came down a long, winding cliff-side road and then headed into a canyon, where the road ran alongside a sparkling river. Below them the water wound through the trees, disappeared, reappeared, the surface glinting in the sun as the road hummed against the tires. They came around a corner to a wide pullout. An old house sat on a hillside across the river, staring down the canyon to the south. Wes pulled in and stopped the car.

"I brought some poles, but we won't go fishing today. Let's get out and stretch, though."

They scrambled down a little path to the water's edge. The river was silent and green, not too high, slipping by with a purpose, heading back down the canyon. The hills lifted above the pines, some of them bare, the red rock outcroppings splashes of blood against the green grass. A little bird sat on a rock in the middle, dipping up and down, watching the water and then plunging in after something it saw. It was the most perfectly lovely place Josie had ever been.

Wes turned to Josie and took her into his arms. She went to him in a rush. She felt like she was blending with him, melting into his being. He looked down at her and then softly bent down to kiss her. And for the first time, Josie could feel what it meant to be loved by a man who loved her with all his heart. He enfolded her in it; he wrapped her in it, and for a moment she felt like she would faint. The feelings and emotions were so strong.

"I love you, Josie. I always have, I always will."

"Wes, oh, Wes. I love you so much. You came for me. You rescued me."

He was silent, and then he just picked her up and carried her to the truck. "We have a few more miles and then we'll be there."

He pulled open the door as he held her and then picked her up and slipped her onto her seat. It was as though she weighed nothing. He went around, climbed in, and they started off. The sun was moving west, dipping behind the canyon wall. They drove for another mile, came around a bend, and suddenly the canyon opened into the most beautiful valley Josie had ever seen. On the right, tall, snow-peaked mountains rose thousands of feet up out of the greenest meadows and fields. On the left side, the valley opened to the East and faded away into a patchwork of green fields and dry hilltops. Josie's mouth was open in wonder. She looked over at Wes. He was taking it in with a smile. "Amanda was right. This is beautiful."

They drove on in silence. They drove through a town called Lostine with an old stone building, The Lostine Tavern, in the middle. A couple of blinks and they were through and back out into the lush farmland. Cattle grazed in the fields. Tall pivot sprinklers sprayed streams of water. Wes pointed to a field. "Look, there are elk in there among the cattle."

Sure enough, a herd of elk was munching grass next to the cows. They passed through the towns of Wallowa, then Enterprise, and then they came to Joseph, Oregon. It was rustic, with bars and shops. They followed the road, bore left and then, after about five miles, they came up over a rise. Wes pulled over, and they both stared at the most beautiful lake they had ever seen. A low glacial moraine ran along the left side above the road and then joined into a mountain that rose thousands of feet into the evening sky. A carpet of wild flowers, blue, red, gold, purple, pink, every color covered the side of the moraine. To the right side of the lake, another wonderful mountain rose straight up out of the water. The lake itself lay in the cup of a bowl that looked like a giant hand had come down from heaven and scooped out a bed for it. It must have been three or four miles long and at the end, the two mountains separated. In the gap, another, even taller mountain, rose above the lake, reflected in the still waters.

Josie turned to Wes. "This is absolutely beautiful, Wes. Stunning."

Wes started up and followed the road that ran along the east side of the lake. They drove all the way down to the end of the lake and as they came around the last bend, a park-like area opened to their sight. In the middle was an old-fashioned lodge, perched on the edge of the lake.

Josie grabbed Wes's arm. "Is this where we are staying?"

Wes nodded. "Yep. This is the place."

"Oh, Wes. How beautiful."

Wes pulled into the parking lot and helped Josie out. He grabbed their suitcases and they went inside. They checked in, made a reservation for dinner, and took their things up to their room. Josie freshened up, and they went down to dinner around seven o'clock. It was unseasonably warm, so they chose a table on the deck overlooking the lake. They sat quietly and ate their dinner. The day was disappearing over the western mountain.

A tiny breeze stirred the last rays of light on the surface of the lake into broken crystals of light. The sun eased toward the top of the mountain, and then the breeze died to nothing. A great peace settled. The dancing diamonds smoothed to green ice. The only sound was the rustling of the tiny waves coming in. The lake was absolutely still and smooth, and they saw the shoreline, and the mountain, a perfect mirror image on the far side.

Nothing moved. It was as though the day was holding its breath. The sun slid behind the ridge, slowly, each piece disappearing into a split in time, into the place where tomorrow lives. The last ray pierced the oranges, the deep pinks, the growing blue. One last rim of light and then it went. A tiny breeze sprang up and the surface of the lake splintered into a million diamond pieces.

Josie took Wes's hand. "Oh, Wes, there must be a God. Something this beautiful doesn't just happen by chance, does it?"

Wes shook his head. "No, honey, it doesn't. There's a psalm in the Bible, Psalm 19. It's one of my favorites." He squeezed her hand and looked up at the night sky, remembering.

"The heavens declare the glory of God;
the skies proclaim the work of His hands.
Day after day they pour forth speech;
night after night they reveal knowledge.
Without speech or language,
without a sound to be heard,
their voice has gone out into all the earth,
their words to the ends of the world."

Josie looked at this Wes, this Wes who loved her and had made her his wife. "Oh, Wes, that's beautiful."

The waitress came and asked if they wanted dessert. They smiled and declined. Wes took Josie's hand, and they went up to their room. And in the hours that followed, Josie Winters, now Josie Branson, found the treasure she had been searching for all her life.

REPRIEVE

My dad told me it was as if the good Lord had given them a reprieve, a golden time where He mended the broken pieces of their lives, and all the dreams that seemed to be gone were opened again, washed clean, and brought out new and sparkling. My mother was pain free for the whole time they were on their honeymoon. They went fishing; they hiked trails into the mountains, they even rode the highest tram in America to the top of the mountain next to the Lodge. But most of all, they spent the fleeting moments rediscovering each other as husband and wife, lovers and, most important, best friends.

Wes took care of Josie and she responded by blooming under his touch. It was a wonderful time and when my dad shared it with me after my mom passed, he cried.

Margi

Chapter Twenty-Two

FINDING THE WAY

The next five days were the most wonderful days of Josie Branson's life. They went fishing at the lake; they hiked up trails into the mountains; they took a tram ride to the top of Mount Howard and had lunch at the restaurant there. Wes was there for her every moment, watching over her, taking care of her, loving her. It was as though God had given her a stay, a timeout from the "It" so she could be with Wes completely. On the last day at the Lodge, they got up very early to watch the sunrise from the east over the moraine. The sun rose from that side in glory, seeking its measured path above the lake to the ridges of Chief Joseph Mountain—the edifice rising beside the lake and going up forever into the pristine blue sky. As they watched, a massive thunderhead rolled in from the west over the mountain, pouring rain at the north end of the lake but not touching them. Just as quickly as it appeared, it faded away, moving across the prairie toward Idaho. The sun came back in brilliance, lighting the fields of flowers on the mountainsides. The fragrance of flowers and the stabbing loveliness of the smell of spring rain flooded her senses. It was as though, with her life winding down, Josie Branson was given a taste of life as it really could be, full to the brim with beauty, kindness, and love. She moved close to Wes and encircled him with her arms.

"Thank you for this, Wes. These days have been life as I always dreamed it would be." She lifted her face, and he leaned down and kissed it.

"I know, Josie, I only wish…"

She reached up and put her finger to his lips. "I know, my darling. And I wish it too. But we have this and when I'm… when I'm gone, you will have this perfect time to remember."

They packed the truck after they checked out and drove out of the parking lot in silence. When they came to the foot of the lake, Wes pulled over and they got out. The lake was perfectly still—the mountain with its spring snowcap reflected perfectly in the mirror surface. Under the image, the rocks at the bottom of the lake created a beautiful marble texture behind the lovely picture. They stood for a long time, hand in hand, and then turned, climbed into the truck, and drove away.

Josie thought she would be sad, but her heart was too full with all the wonder she had experienced. She moved over on the bench seat and got under Wes's arm. They didn't say a word for many miles, both lost in their thoughts.

IT WAS early evening when they arrived back home. There was a note on the door and a box on the porch. The note was from Amanda and simply said, 'Welcome home.' Inside the box was some fried chicken and potato salad. The chicken was still warm.

Wes grinned and picked up the box. "Let's go eat on the deck."

Josie looked at him, puzzled. "What deck?"

"Our new deck."

She followed him around the side of the house. Under the big maple tree, there was a beautiful new wooden deck. It had a screened arbor with a roof and open sides. A wrought iron rail went all the way around, with an opening on the side toward the house. There was a picnic table and some Adirondack chairs with big cushions. A gas barbecue sat toward the back. Josie's jaw dropped.

"When...?"

Then she saw something she hadn't noticed at first. In the corner of the deck was a big pot. In the pot was a large, almost fully grown, honeysuckle plant. Blossoms covered it. As Josie watched, she heard a strange whirring noise. A little bird appeared as if by magic. It was a hummingbird! Josie watched as the little bird flitted from blossom to blossom. From out of nowhere, another little bird joined it. Together, they sought the nectar in the flowers. Then, just like they appeared, they were gone.

"Wes... hummingbirds."

He nodded and smiled. "I had some local guys build this while we were gone. I thought we should have a place to sit out and watch the birds and the sky, enjoy some barbecue. I found that honeysuckle plant when I was out one day. It reminded me... well, of some good times we had a long time ago. I hoped they would come, but I honestly didn't think the hummers would be here so soon."

"You built this for me, Wes?"

He nodded and took her in his arms. "I want you to have the most wonderful time before... before..." He choked up.

Josie reached up and touched his face. "It's okay, honey. We'll play the hand we're dealt."

———

THE DAYS PASSED QUICKLY after that. The "It" came back and slowly Josie could feel the life in her fading. She wasn't hungry as much. Her skin lost its healthy glow, and she slept more and more.

Dr. Gary helped as much as he could, monitoring her medications. The deck became a haven for Josie. Set under the shade of the giant maple tree, it stayed cool even on hotter days. She delighted in the hummingbirds who came every day. Wes hung a feeder on one of the roof posts, and soon there were at least four of the beautiful little birds darting about.

As the days moved toward early summer, it was harder and harder for Josie to sit up, so Wes got a hospital bed and they set it up outside. He sat by her every day, talking to her, joking with her, watching her as she slept.

One evening, Josie woke to find Wes sitting beside her, crying. She reached out and touched his cheek.

"I'm sorry, Wes. I'm sorry for you, my darling. What will you do when I'm gone?"

"I don't know, Josie, I don't know."

Then she asked the question, the one for which she had no answer. "I'm afraid, Wes. What will happen to me when I die? Is there a heaven up there for worn out old cowgirls?"

Wes took her hand. "Can I tell you a story, my darling girl?"

She nodded.

"Remember when I told you about Steve, when he sent me to take Luis to the medics?"

"Yes, you said he had the most peaceful look on his face—he told you he wasn't afraid to die."

"Yes, and even when I came back and found him dead, that look of peace was still there. I wondered what it was, what he had that I didn't have. I was so afraid to die, and yet I was still alive and he wasn't, but he had gone willingly to save me and Luis.

"When I got out of the hospital, I went back to the aid station to find out about Luis. No one could tell me where they took him. After about a week I found out they sent him to the big hospital at Red Beach Base near Danang, but a couple of days after I got out of the hospital, the marines discharged me and shipped me out, so I never got over there. I guess He was there for four or five months before they sent him home. I looked for Luis when I got stateside, tried to get a line on him, but I couldn't track him down.

"I didn't know he was still in Nam and I didn't know any of his relatives' names, so I was at a dead end. I searched for Luis Hidalgo for a long time, almost ten years. Finally, I remembered my captain, Doug, was assigned to the VA department in Washington. I wrote him a letter. He wrote back in a month and said he tracked Luis down, but he couldn't give me his information since it was confidential. But he said he would write Luis and send him my address, and if Luis wanted, he could write me."

"So, you found him?"

"Yeah. He got the letter from my captain, and he wrote back to me. I got a letter about six weeks after I talked to Doug. Luis was in the Dallas VA facility. He had been there since he came home and he's still there. He had suffered a very traumatic head wound in the firefight and he had PTSD, so he couldn't really function in the world. I was in Texas when I got his letter, so it was easy for me to get up to Dallas. Luis was glad to see me, and it was good to see him."

"What happened when you told him about Steve?"

"You know, that was the strange thing. At first, I was reluctant to tell him, given his PTSD, but after he dug the story out of me, it didn't seem to bother him. When I told him about the peace Steve had, he even smiled. He said he wouldn't expect anything else from him."

Josie knit her brows. "What was it about Steve, then? Luis knew?"

"That's what I asked him. He told me that Steve had a powerful faith in God. I was surprised, because in my alcohol haze, I must have missed that. Well, I had to think about that because I never went to church, or had anybody tell me anything about faith. I guess I needed to find out what it was about. I had Steve's address, so after I left Luis, I went to see Steve's mom."

Josie was very interested now. "What did she say?"

"She agreed with Luis. Told me that Steve had grown up a believer and had never lost his faith, even when most of his childhood friends had. As we talked, I realized that I must have suspected something like this about Steve, but we had never talked about it. He didn't shove religion down people's throats, he just lived it in front of them. He was a different kind of guy. When I thought back, I remembered that I never heard him cuss or tell an off-color joke. He always treated women, even the B-Girls in Saigon, with respect. When we went to a bar, he would have one beer, maybe two, but I never saw him drunk. I realized at that moment Steve had something that was missing in my life."

"So, what did you do?"

"I talked to Steve's mom a long time about it. I stayed with her for a few days. She helped me understand what it was about. She bought me a Bible. After that I tried to learn what I could about having a relationship with God, and with His Son."

"You mean, Jesus?"

"Yes."

"Is Jesus real, Wes? I used to think so when I was young and... unspoiled."

"Well, honey, He is real. After everything that's happened to me, and everything I've tried, to find peace with myself, He's the only thing that makes any sense."

"And that's why you came here?"

Wes took Josie's hands in his. "I came because it was a chance for me to be a man, a real man. And I had to search my heart before I came to make sure what I was doing wasn't about me. It would have been real easy for me to do something that made me feel good about myself. I had to get past that. I had to find the place in my heart where everything I did was for you, and only for you. And then, and only then, could I come."

Josie shook her head. "So, you came because..."

"Because I love you, Josie. You're the only girl I have ever loved. From the moment I saw you at the fair that night, to this moment, that has never changed. I've always known I loved you, but I had to find a way to make that real for you, too. I believe He has helped me do that."

Josie looked up at Wes, into his eyes. There was nothing there but love, genuine love. She could feel it. "I need to think about this, Wes."

Chapter Twenty-Three

WHEN THE HUMMINGBIRDS DANCED

"Play me the song, Wes."

"Hummingbirds?"

"Yes. I haven't heard it in so long. And I haven't heard you sing it since you got here."

Wes shrugged. "Yeah, I guess I put it away a long time ago."

"Will you play it for me?"

He nodded. "Let me go get my guitar."

It was a lovely June afternoon, almost evening. The weather had been steady in the 70s for a couple of weeks. Josie spent a lot of time out on the deck, propped up on her bed. Wes had some netting up so flies and bugs did not bother his girl. Josie watched him walk to the trailer.

He's so beautiful. A man's man. I love him so...

She felt the dull ache in her side, pain she knew was numbed by the morphine, but still there. She had spent the last week feeling the life slowly drain out of her. She had no appetite, was not even thirsty, and slept a lot. Except for taking care of Salty and keeping some weeds out of the driveway, Wes was by her side every minute. During this last week, Josie had shared her fears, her delights, her regrets, and Wes let her know that he was there only for her. The one thing she had not talked to Wes about was her death—and about the conversation they had about his friend Steve.

She had been thinking hard and long about what he said. And she realized she did not know what would happen to her after she closed her eyes for the last time. She knew that anything she hoped might happen to her when she died was just wishful thinking. She had no certainty, no absolute truth to cling to, no life preserver for her soul.

She heard the whirring of the hummingbird wings.

Two, three... where's Tiny?

Then the fourth hummer appeared. Two of them, the male and the female adults, chased each other. They went up into the maple and then back to the honeysuckle. They whirled around each other in a dance.

The hummingbirds danced the day we met. I was a town girl, he was a rodeo cowboy. We met at the Laredo / Webb County Fourth of July Fair in the summer of 1962. I was at the animal barn, wandering from stall to stall, looking at the horses and dreaming. I didn't come to the fair with them. I didn't want to be around my mom and Ted. I wanted to enjoy the fair without her vapid, gossipy comments and the unwanted touches from him. I rode the bus all the way from the other side of town...

I was looking at the horses and wondering what it would be like to own one. Wes came up behind me and asked me if I liked horses. At first I thought he was a perv, but when I turned to look, oh my, he stole my heart. He was so handsome. Dark hair, chiseled face, blue eyes to die for. Oh, Wes...

That night, we started the song. The sky was beautiful... gold, pink, blue, purple, rose, orange... a honeysuckle sky. I watched the hummingbirds dance. Way up into the sky.

She heard him slip into his chair. She turned on the bed. It took an effort of her will. Her body was rebellious these days. She would send it directions from her head and it would just do what it wanted, anyway. He smiled and opened the guitar case. She watched his hands, so big, powerful, but gentle as he took out the old Martin D28, slipped the strap over his shoulder.

"I haven't played since before we went on our honeymoon."

"When you first got here, I went out to your trailer one night to tell you to go. You were working on a song."

He blushed.

Strange. He's such a man, and yet he blushes so easily.

"You heard that?"

"Yes, it was sweet. Play it for me."

"It's not done yet."

"Please, play what you have."

He nodded. Strummed a chord then...

They were good days

Sweet times

Hot summer nights and

Dream times

Layin' in the grass

With my head in the stars

There was promise in your kiss

And forever in your arms

His rich baritone thrilled her. "That's going to be a beautiful song, Wes. You remember those days?"

"Josie, those days are with me like my skin. They used to weigh on me like a millstone, but since we got married, I feel like those days have been redeemed... at least a little."

She put her hand on his. "They have been, my darling. You have saved me." She looked away for a moment. "Well, at least in this life. I... I don't know what happens after this."

"Have you been thinking about what we talked about?"

"I have, but I don't really understand it all. Can you tell me?" Wes nodded.

"Help me sit up, then. I don't want to fall asleep."

Wes leaned the guitar up against the railing, helped her, then took a deep breath. "I'm not a preacher, and I didn't go to Bible school, but I've done a little studying on my own, and asked some questions of a pastor I know in Texas. First, let me ask if you have any questions."

Josie thought for a moment. "Well, from what I remember, it seems like what Christians believe is that there is this being, this God, who is up in the sky that says, 'If you don't do what I say, I'll send you to hell.' At least that's what the people in the church I went to when I was a little girl thought. I mean, all the time they were making up rules and regulations they made everyone live by so they wouldn't lose their salvation. But at the same time, they talked about the grace of God and how God loved the world. Seems like you could get pretty mixed up."

Wes nodded. "Yep, whenever men stick in their two cents, everything gets SNAFU."

"SNAFU?"

"It's a term the Marines use. It means 'Situation normal, all... all fouled up.'"

Josie grinned. "I've heard a different word in there."

"Yeah, well, I'm trying to smooth out some of the old Marine that pops up every once in a while." They both laughed.

"Anyway, I discovered two things. Number one, I needed God in my life, but I didn't know why, and two, the only way to find out the truth about him was to read the Bible."

"Isn't the Bible just another book about how to be good? I mean, you can't take it literal, can you?"

"Actually, there are more ancient manuscripts confirming what the Bible says than any other book in the world, including all the Greek classics and the great writings of the past. I have found it to be trustworthy."

"So, what does it say then, I mean about us and... God? I mean, who needs a God that sends us to hell if we don't obey him?"

"Actually, He doesn't. Our problem is we are broken from the moment we are born. We are on the way to hell all on our own. How do we know that? Because we... we... we all die. Death is the surest indicator that something is not right between us and God." Wes looked away and wiped his eyes. Then he turned back and took Josie's hand. "Everybody dies, all of us. In the Bible, it says that God planned for us to live with him forever and never die. But we blew it, and since then we have not only done a bunch of rotten things we need to pay for, but we are also just basically rotten inside. It's who we are. And there is a reason for that, but I'm trying to keep this simple, understandable." Wes took another breath.

"God, because He is perfect in all His ways, can't be around us in the condition we are in. So, He offers a remedy. The life of His Son in exchange for ours. Every crime has a consequence and there is a price to pay. So instead of making us pay for it, He asked His Son to take the punishment on our behalf. Just like Steve died for me and Luis, that's what Jesus did for all of us when He willingly went to die on the cross. It was a gift of love. And the wonderful thing is that we don't have to earn it. He gives it to us because He loves us. All we need to do is believe that's what He did for us and when the time comes, we saddle up and ride on into heaven. And after that, death has no more power over us—God accepts us because of what His son did. And that's as simple as I can make it."

Josie was silent for a long time, thinking about it. She sighed. "Do you believe that, Wes?"

"I surely do."

"And that's why you came here, to tell me?"

"It is. I figured maybe I could tell you better just by helping you, loving you, for no other reason than to show you God's love through me. I hope I did."

Josie took a deep breath. "You showed me love, Wes. Love like I have never known. I don't really understand it, but I'm willing to take you at your word." She felt tears start in her eyes. "Do you think, do you think, He could love me, Wes? I've done so many rotten things, wretched things. Could He love even me?"

"He sure can."

And then, like waking up, she remembered riding in the car on her wedding day. The silent question she asked when she whispered. "Why do you love me?"

And it was a question for Wes, and for Amanda, and for whoever or whatever was revealing itself to her in that moment. And she remembered the answer, like a still, small voice.

I just do.

And then the light came on in Josie Branson's heart. She reached up for Wes. He came to her and pulled her into him. She was crying. "I remember, Wes. On our wedding day. He spoke to me, Wes, in the car. He told me He loved me, loved me for no reason, except He just did. Oh, Wes, I remember... I heard Him speak to me. It was Him, I know it was. Oh, I believe you, Wes. I believe you."

Wes's arms tightened around her and she felt his love and the love that was flowing through him to her and Josie knew finally and for sure that she never had to be afraid again.

They stayed that way for a long time, then she smiled up at him and lay back.

"Play the song for me, Wes."

He picked up the guitar and began to play and sing.

When the hummingbirds danced in a honeysuckle sky
And the stars fell down on the fourth of July
She never knew about love 'til she saw it in his eyes
When the hummingbirds danced in a honeysuckle sky

HE WAS a buckaroo cowboy with a dollar in his pocket,
She was a little-town girl with an old silver locket.
He told her that he loved her and they talked all night
and all her dreams came true when he held her so tight

. . .

When the hummingbirds danced in a honeysuckle sky
    And the stars fell down on the fourth of July
    She never knew about love 'til she saw it in his eyes
    When the hummingbirds danced in a honeysuckle sky

There's nothing like love when it comes like a twister
    She was so sweet well he couldn't resist her
    A man makes a promise and a woman says yes
    now she's a wife named Josie with a hubby called Wes

When the hummingbirds danced in a honeysuckle sky
    And the stars fell down on the fourth of July
    She never knew about love 'til she saw it in his eyes
    When the hummingbirds danced in a honeysuckle sky

Sweet dreams and colors in the sky
    will you still be with me when the hummingbirds fly
    I'm counting' on you baby, cause I can't go let go
    Just keep on lovin' me, please keep loving me
    Tell me that you love me, and we'll never say goodbye

When the hummingbirds danced in a honeysuckle sky
    And the stars fell down on the fourth of July
    She never knew about love 'til she saw it in his eyes
    When the hummingbirds danced in a honeysuckle sky

. . .

WHEN HE FINISHED, Wes looked at his wife. Her eyes were closed. He touched her face. It was cool. He put the guitar down and took her wrist in his hands, feeling for the pulse, but there was none.

Josie was gone.

Wes held her hand for a long time, bent over her, silent sobs shaking his body, tears running down his face.

Above Wes, the evening turned to gold, then rose, then blue and orange. There was a whirring sound and then Josie's hummingbirds were hovering just above Josie and Wes. Slowly, like a ballet, they danced together, spiraling higher and higher until they disappeared into the honeysuckle sky.

THE REST OF THE STORY — MARGI

After my mother died, I got a letter from Wes, my dad. Josie had left him her little ranchette in her will and he had decided to stay there. He got a job cowboying for a local ranch and he asked me to bring my boy and come live with him. I thought about it for a week, and then I decided I should go. There was nothing for me in Laredo, so I put my grandma's house on the market and was surprised when it sold rather quickly. I packed my things and headed for Bend, Oregon.

And so, on an August day almost exactly a year after my mother drove into a little town in Oregon on her last adventure, I drove into Bend in my old car, a U-Haul full of stuff and my six-year-old son, Billy. I drove out to Josie's place. When I got there, I found my dad working on the gingerbread trim on the front porch. The place was immaculate. Wes had it looking like a park.

I was shy when I got out of the car. So was Billy. But Wes just shook his hand and said, "Howdy, pard," and after that, they were almost inseparable. My dad greeted me with a hug and as I looked into his eyes, I knew my mom had been right to marry him. Wes was a what-you-see-is-what-you-get kind of guy. There were no hidden agendas. He was a real man. And in that moment, I was real glad I had come. It was coming home.

Billy took to Wes like a duck to water. Within a day or two, Grandpa had him up on Salty and the two were riding out on the prairie, Billy on Salty and Wes on a beautiful brown cutting horse he bought at the auction.

Well, it's been twenty-five years since my mom died. About five years after I came, the neighbor next door left and sold his property to Wes—forty acres. We raised cattle and sheep and had a profitable side business.

Last week I was with Wes when he passed away. He was a great father to me and helped me raise my Billy to be a veterinarian and a cowboy. Billy learned about animals right on our place and now he has a practice here in Bend.

Before he died, I brought Wes home from the hospital and I was with Wes every day until he passed. During those few days, he was alert and present and he shared many things with me about the eight months He and Josie spent together.

On the day he died, he had the most peaceful look on his face. "I'm not afraid to die, Margi. And I know she'll be waiting for me when I cross over. She went on ahead, but I never stopped loving her. And when I'm there with her, I know we'll be watching the hummingbirds dance in heaven's honeysuckle sky..."

Margi

Patrick E. Craig is an award-winning author with twenty-two published novels. He has won seven CIBA Book Awards, a Selah Award and a Word Guild Book Award. His work includes three Amish mysteries, six Amish novels, three World War II historical novels with a short story sequel, two anthologies of Amish stories, a standalone novel and a memoir, two YA paranormal books, and this book, a redemptive romance. He lives in Idaho with his wife Judy.

MORE BOOKS BY PATRICK E. CRAIG

A Quilt For Jenna

The Road Home

Jenny's Choice

The Amish Heiress

The Amish Princess

The Mennonite Queen

The Journals of Jenny Hershberger

The Mystery of Ghost Dancer Ranch

The Lost Coast

The Gettysburg Letter

The Amish Menorah and Other Stories

A Christmas Collection

Say Goodbye To The River

Far On The Ringing Plains

The Scepter And The Isle

Men Who Strove With Gods

Beyond The Red Hills

The Drive

The Honor Trail

The Quilt That Knew

The Boy In Blue Denim

3 X 3

Contact Patrick at pec@patrickecraig.com

Patrick's Website: https://pjpublishing.biz/

Patrick's Amazon Author Page: https://tinyurl.com/y3nwsmgs

THE PORCH SWING MYSTERIES

Book 1—The Quilt That Knew

CHANTICLEER INTERNATIONAL BOOK AWARDS FIRST PLACE WINNER — MYSTERY & MAYHEM FOR COZY AND NOT SO COZY MYSTERIES

• A young girl buried in the woods for forty years...

• A desperate killer loose in the village...

• A mysterious quilt and a golden ring...

Jenny Hershberger returns to Apple Creek, Ohio, the village where she grew up. But this is not a happy homecoming. She's been called upon to solve a horrible crime. But will the killer find her first...

Book 2—The Boy In Blue Denim

CHANTICLEER INTERNATIONAL BOOK AWARDS FIRST PLACE WINNER — MYSTERY & MAYHEM FOR COZY AND NOT SO COZY MYSTERIES

• A young boy murdered in a snowstorm and forgotten...

• A mysterious letter that sets Jenny on the trail...

• Secrets within secrets revealed - nothing is as it seems...

Imagine if Miss Marple were Amish!

Jenny Hershberger returns to Apple Creek, Ohio, called by Detective Elbert Wainwright to help solve another cold case—a young Amish boy murdered in a deadly snowstorm and never identified. But as she digs into the case, she finds so many connections to her own life that the story becomes like a house of mirrors. As Jenny and Bobby Halverson travel from Apple Creek to Shipshewana, to Texas and Colorado, and back to Apple Creek, the trail grows warmer each day. But each step uncovers a new murder... and a new twist. Who is the killer? And who is... **THE BOY IN BLUE DENIM?**

Book 3—3 X 3

Jenny Hershberger is the most unusual amateur sleuth, winning hearts with her courage, compassion, and ability to think outside the box... Reader's Favorite Review

Jenny Hershberger has returned to Apple Creek, the small Amish Village in Wayne County, Ohio, where she spent her childhood. She purchased her family home and hopes to find peace there.

But then a horrific new mystery comes her way. Three random killings, all marked by the bloody signature of a ruthless serial killer, electrify the little town of Wooster, Ohio. Elbert Wainwright, Jenny's counterpart on the Wooster police force, puts his team to work and quickly hunts down the man they think is responsible—a mentally disabled Vietnam War vet. All the evidence points to Steven Lambright.

But when Elbert calls Jenny and her old friend, retired Sheriff Bobby Halverson, to help, the case against Lambright starts to go south as Jenny discovers there is much more to the story than meets the eye. One by one, Jenny uncovers secrets hidden for forty years, secrets deeply connected to the Amish community. And as she brings them to light, Jenny finds the past can reveal much about the present—in terrifying ways.

THE APPLE CREEK DREAMS SERIES

Book 1—A Quilt For Jenna

Jerusha Springer has spent months making the most beautiful quilt anyone in Apple Creek, Ohio has ever seen, and she knows it is going to take first prize at the Quilt Fair in Dalton. The prize money will be her ticket out of the Amish way of life—away from the memories of Jenna, the daughter she lost a year ago and Reuben, her tormented husband, who has been missing since Jenna's death.

On the way to the fair, Jerusha gets caught in the Storm of The Century. An accident leaves her trapped in her driver's car—and trapped by the memories of her marriage to Reuben and the loss of little Jenna. And then another littler girl enters the story and takes Jerusha's heart captive in a way she hadn't expected. Can this child also be the one to heal Reuben's pain as well?

A beautiful story of loss and redemption.

Book 2—The Road Home

Author Patrick Craig continues the story of Jenny Springer, the child rescued in A Quilt for Jenna, with a story of reconciliation and healing.

Jenny Springer is the local historian for the Amish community in Apple Creek, Ohio. When Jenny was a child, Jerusha Hershberger Springer rescued her from a terrible snowstorm, and when no trace of Jenny's parents could be found, the Springer family adopted her. Since then, the burning desire in Jenny's heart is to find out who she really is.

Then Jenny meets Jonathan Hershberger, a drifter from San Francisco who lands in Apple Creek fleeing a drug deal gone wrong. Intrigued by an *Englischer* with an Amish name, Jenny offers to help him discover his Amish roots. When together they dig into Jonathan's past, Jenny gets serious in her own search for her long-lost parents. And as they travel The Road Home together, Jenny finds the truly surprising answer to her deepest questions, while Jonathan discovers his need for a home, a family, and a relationship with God.

Book 3—*Jenny's Choice*

Jonathan and Jenny Hershberger are happily settled in Paradise, Pennsylvania on the farm Jenny inherited from her grandfather. But when Jonathan disappears in a terrible boating accident, Jenny and her young daughter, Rachel, return home to Apple Creek, Ohio to live with her adoptive parents, Reuben and Jerusha Springer.

As Jenny works through her grief and despair, she discovers she has a gift for writing. A handsome young publisher discovers her work and, after the publication of her first book, Jenny is on the verge of worldly success and possible romance.

Then a conflict arises with the elders of her church, and Jenny must ask herself if she's willing to go outside her faith to pursue her dreams. At the same time, the budding romance is at odds with Jenny's hope that Jonathan might someday be found alive. Jenny must choose and Jenny's Choice leads her to the surprising and heart-warming conclusion of the Apple Creek Dreams series.

THE PARADISE CHRONICLES SERIES

Book 1—The Amish Heiress

Rachel Hershberger's life in Paradise, Pennsylvania is far from happy. Her papa struggles with a terrible event from the past, and his emotional instability has created an irreparable breach between them. Rachel's one desire is to leave the Amish way of life and Paradise forever. Then her prayers are answered. Rachel discovers that the strange, key-shaped birthmark above her heart identifies her as the heiress to a vast fortune left by her *Englischer* grandfather, Robert St. Clair. If Rachel will marry a suitable descendent of the St. Clair family, she will inherit an enormous sum of money. But Rachel does not know that behind the scenes is her long-dead grandfather's sister-in-law, Augusta St. Clair, a vicious woman who will do anything to keep the fortune in her own hands. As the deceptions and intrigues of the St. Clair family bind her in their web, Rachel realizes that she has made a terrible mistake. But has her change of heart come too late?

Book 2—The Amish Princess

Opahtuhwe, the White Deer, is the beautiful daughter of Wingenund, the powerful chief of the Delaware tribe, and a true princess. Everything in her life changes when the renegade known as Scar brings three Amish prisoners to the Delaware camp. Jonathan and Joshua Hershberger are twin brothers that Scar has determined to adopt and teach the Indian way. The third prisoner is Jonas Hershberger, their father, who has been made a slave because he would not defend his family. White Deer is drawn to Jonathan but his hatred of the Indians makes him push her away. Joshua's gentle heart and steadfast refusal to abandon the Amish faith lead White Deer to a life-changing decision, and rejection by her people. In the end, White Deer must choose between the ways of her people and her new-found faith. And complicating it all is her love for the man who can only hate her.

Book 3—The Mennonite Queen

CHANTICLEER INTERNATIONAL BOOK AWARDS SEMI-FINALIST - THE CHAUCER HISTORICAL DIVISION: This is the third book in The Paradise Chronicles series. Isabella, Princess of Poland, is raised to a life of great wealth and leisure in the Polish Royal Court, destined to marry a king. But fate or divine providence intervenes when she meets Johan Hirschberg, a young Anabaptist who works in her father's stable. This chance meeting leads the young couple into a forbidden love. Together they flee Poland and embark on a dangerous journey that brings them, after great peril, to the small parish of a troubled priest named Menno Simons. Catholic Bishop, Franz von Waldek, paid by King Sigismund, Isabella's father to find the princess at all costs, pursues them across Europe. Isabella does not know it, but if von Waldek captures her, she will have to make a choice that will change the course of European history forever.

THE ISLANDS SERIES

Book 1—Far On The Ringing Plains

CHANTICLEER INTERNATIONAL BOOK AWARDS FIRST PLACE WINNER — HEMINGWAY 20TH CENTURY WARTIME FICTION.

FAR ON THE RINGING PLAINS — INSPIRED BY TRUE EVENTS In the spirit of The Thin Red Line, Hacksaw Ridge, Flags of our Fathers and Pearl Harbor. Realistic. Gritty. Gutsy. Without taking it too far, Craig and Pura take it far enough to bring war home to your heart, mind, and soul. The rough edge of combat is here. And the rough edge of language, human passion, and our flawed humanity. If you can handle the ruggedness and honesty of Saving Private Ryan, 1917 or Dunkirk, you can handle the power and authenticity of ISLANDS: Far on the Ringing Plains. For the beauty and the honor is here too. Just like the Bible, in all its roughness and realism and truthfulness about life, reaching out for God is ever-present in ISLANDS. So are hope and faith and self-sacrifice. Prayer. Christ. Courage. An indomitable spirit. And the best of human nature, triumphing over the worst. Bud Parmalee, Johnny Strange, Billy Martens—three men that had each other's backs and the backs of every Marine in their company and platoon. All three were raised never to fight. All three saw no other choice but to enlist and try to make a difference. All three would never be the same again. Never. And neither would their world. This is their story.

Book 2—The Scepter and The Isle

CHANTICLEER INTERNATIONAL BOOK AWARDS FINALIST — HEMINGWAY 20TH CENTURY WARTIME FICTION

It did not end with Guadalcanal. It did not end with one island. There were more islands... an island with snow-capped peaks, friendly people, blue seas, where Bud found love with his Tongan princess. Where Billy breathed the clean air of mountains where no danger lurked. Where Johnny found a way to drain the hate that drove him mad. They found life again after the death-filled frenzy of Guadalcanal But the God of war was not done with them. More islands sent their siren call from beyond distant horizons and they were cast upon dark shores. Islands with coconut palms, dense green jungle and death. Islands that took more life than they ever gave back. Islands where women killed like men, islands filled with the most brutal soldiers the Japanese Empire could offer. Tarawa. Saipan. Islands that had to be endured. Islands they had to survive. There was no other way to bring the war to an end. There was no other way to get home again.

Book 3—Men Who Stove With Gods

CHANTICLEER INTERNATIONAL BOOK AWARDS FINALIST — HEMINGWAY 20TH CENTURY WARTIME FICTION

 Since 1941 the Marines have fought the Japanese. They met them first on Guadalcanal, a maelstrom of death and fury. Tarawa, Saipan, Okinawa—their friends died beside them, their youth disappeared in a baptism of fire, but they kept on. Johnny, Bud, and Billy went ashore on bloodstained Okinawa hungry for the end of the war. But they knew when the battle ended, they would face their Armageddon on the sacred beaches of Japan.

9 798987 145180